THE PYRAMID

▲

THE
PYRAMID

ISMAIL KADARE

*Translated from the French
of Jusuf Vrioni by David Bellos,
in consultation with the author*

ARCADE PUBLISHING · NEW YORK

FIRST ARCADE PAPERBACK EDITION

First published in France under the title *La pyramide*
(Albanian title, *Pluhuri mbretëror*)

This edition is based on the second (1993) French edition

This is a work of fiction. Names, places, characters, and incidents are either the
products of the author's imagination or are used fictitiously.

Library of Congress Cataloging-in-Publication Data

Kadare, Ismail.
      [Pluhuri mbretëror. English]
      The pyramid / Ismail Kadare ; translated from the French of Jusuf Vrioni by
David Bellos. —1st Arcade paperback ed.
          p. cm.
      Originally published in Albanian.
      ISBN 1-55970-314-8 (hc)
      ISBN 1-55970-791-7 (pb)
      1. Great Pyramid (Egypt)—Fiction. I. Bellos, David. II. Vrioni, Jusuf.
III. Title.
      PG9621.K6P5813 1996
      891'.9913—dc20   95–17859

Published in the United States by Arcade Publishing, Inc., New York
Distributed by Time Warner Book Group

Visit our Web site at www.arcadepub.com

10 9 8 7 6 5 4 3 2 1

Designed by API

EB

PRINTED IN THE UNITED STATES OF AMERICA

CONTENTS

▲

I

Origins

An Old Idea Resurrected with Difficulty

WHEN, one morning in late autumn, only a few months after he had ascended the throne of Egypt, Cheops, the new Pharaoh, let slip that he might perhaps not wish to have a pyramid erected for him, all who heard him—the palace astrologer, some of the most senior ministers, Cheops's old counselor Userkaf, and the High Priest Hemiunu, who also held the post of architect-in-chief—furrowed their brows as if they had just heard news of a catastrophe.

The courtiers held back for a moment, scouring the sovereign's countenance in the hope of discerning in it a trace of irony, and then (as each would tell the story later on) they tried to take heart from the "perhaps" that the Pharaoh had muttered. But Cheops's visage remained impenetrable, and the courtiers' hope that his words had been just one of those frivolous pronouncements that young monarchs entertain themselves with over a luncheon became increasingly threadbare. Had he not had two of Egypt's most ancient temples closed down just a few weeks before? And then ordered the posting of a decree that forbade Egyptians to indulge henceforth in sacrificial practices?

Cheops was also trying to plumb their expressions. An ironic glimmer in his eye seemed to be asking: Does that distress you so much? As if it were not my pyramid, but yours! O Re, see how servility has already marked their faces! How will it be in years to come when I shall be older and harsher?

Without saying a word, without even according them a glance, he rose and left.

As soon as they were alone, they turned anxiously to face each other. What has befallen us? they whispered. What is this misfortune? One of the ministers took ill and had to lean on the wall of the balcony. The High Priest had tears in his eyes.

The spirals of sand stirred up by the wind shimmered outside. With bewilderment on their faces they gazed at these vortices reaching toward the heavens. They stayed silent, and only their eyes appeared to say: By what stairway wilt thou rise on high, O our sovereign? When the day comes, how wilt thou climb to the firmament, there to change in your turn into a star, like all other Pharaohs? How wilt thou illuminate us?

They spoke among themselves softly, then went their different ways. Two of them went to seek an audience with Khentkaus, the sovereign's mother; another went to get drunk; the craftiest went down to the cellars where the old archives were kept, so as to find old Ipu, the one-eyed scribe.

▲

For the rest of the autumn no one spoke again about the pyramid, not even at the ambassadors' reception, where Cheops, intoxicated with drink, let out things that it is not fitting for a monarch to mention in the presence of foreigners.

The others to whom he had confided his plan nursed the hope that it was just a joke, and even sometimes thought that it was probably better not to allude to it again, as if the idea, if it were no longer stirred, would just sink into the sand by itself. But the opposite hypothesis was so fearful that they thought of nothing else, night and day, save the means of preparing themselves to deal with it.

Some still set great store by the Queen Mother, despite the absence of any encouraging sign from her quarter, while the majority pursued their research in the archives.

The more they burrowed, the harder their work became. A good many papyri had been lost, others were damaged, and even the extant scrolls contained obliterated and excised passages, often with a marginal note "By Order of On High," or indeed without any note at all.

All the same, even the truncated papyri provided them with all kinds of information relating to the object of their search. There was almost everything about the pyramids: their prefiguration in the early tombs called mastabas, the history of the first pyramid, of the second, of the fifth, of their successive alterations, the increase in the size of the base, of their height, the secret embalming formula, the first attempts at robbery, the plans intended to halt such profanation, various accounts of the haulage of the stones, of the granite blocks used to close off the entrances, decrees elevating this or that foreman to this or that rank, death sentences, sketches that were either incomprehensible or specially drawn so as not to be decipherable, etc.

All that was more or less straightforward, but the main aim of their research continued obstinately to escape their grasp among the jungle of papyri, though it winked at them here and there before disappearing again, like a scorpion bolting into a hole. They were hunting for the idea that had led to the conception of pyramids, the secret reason for their existence: and that was what kept on eluding them. It was hidden mainly in obliterated papyrus fragments, and it only ever surfaced from them for an instant at a time.

They had never previously been obliged to engage in such mental effort, and it gave them headaches. However, although the aim of their quest forever eluded them, they ended up finding its outline. If not the thing itself, then at least its shadow.

They debated at length on all that referred to it and, to their great surprise, realized that they were already perfectly aware of what they had been looking for. They had always been privy to the main point, the first principle, of the pyramid's raison d'être, except that it had lain in their minds in a preverbal, indeed in an unthinking state. The papyri of the archives had only draped it in words and in meaning. Insofar as a shadow can be draped.

"All that is perfectly clear," said the High Priest during their last caucus meeting before their audience with the Pharaoh. "We already know what's at the bottom of the problem, or else we would not have been so horrified when the sovereign uttered those words that I do not wish to recall ever again."

Two days later, looking grave and exhausted by insomnia, they were received by Cheops. The Pharaoh was no less

4

somber than they were. For a brief instant a breath of doubt made them wonder if the sovereign might have forgotten the whole business and if they were about to blow on embers to no purpose. But when the High Priest had uttered the words, "We have come to discuss with you the remark that you made concerning the construction of your pyramid," Cheops showed neither amazement nor surprise, and did not even interject: "You mean to say?"

All he did was to sketch a nod of his head that meant: "I am listening!" So they then began to speak, the High Priest first, the others following in turn.

They gave a lengthy, laborious account of all that they had learned from their reading of the papyri, ceaselessly tortured by the idea that they might say more, or less, than was prudent. They spoke of the first pyramid erected by the Pharaoh Zoser, which was only twenty-five cubits high, then of the anger of Pharaoh Sekhemkhet, who had his architect horsewhipped when the plans were laid out, since his pyramid seemed too low for his liking. Then they gave details of the changes made to later plans, in particular by the architect Imhotep, and spoke of the galleries, the burial chamber, the secret passages, and the granite blocks obstructing their entrances, of the three pyramids that Seneferu had had built, one of which had an arris almost five hundred cubits long and a height of three hundred, which you could call truly breathtaking.

Each figure they quoted made them expect to be interrupted—what do such details matter to me!—and they were counting on it so much that, seeing that no interruption came, the High Priest added hoarsely: "Perhaps you are wondering, What have all these facts got to do with me? And you would be right . . . Perhaps they are indeed superfluous for you, but they were only by way of introduction to the heart of the matter."

Encouraged by the sovereign's silence, they expatiated at greater length than they had foreseen on the fundamental aspect of the question. Without making any slip at all, they explained that, according to their research, and although pyramids were indeed magnificent burial places, the idea of building them had, to begin with, no connection with tombs or with death. It had sprung up on its own, that is to say independently of these two notions, and its association with them had been a matter of the merest chance.

For the first time a twitch in Cheops's face gave a sign of life. To their great joy he nodded and mumbled: "Strange!"

"Indeed," the High Priest emphasized. "Many of the things we shall tell you will seem strange to you."

He took such a deep breath that his bloodless old lungs hurt.

"The idea of the pyramids, your Majesty, was born in a period of crisis."

The High Priest was aware of the importance of pausing between sentences. Pauses give greater weight and elevation to thoughts, just as the shade on women's eyelids intensifies the mystery of their glance.

"So it was in a period of crisis," he continued after a moment. "Pharaonic power, as the chronicles record, had been weakened. It was probably not a new phenomenon. The old papyri are full of such turns of fate. What was new at that time was something quite different. The cause of the crisis was unheard of, strange, indeed quite baffling. An unprecedented, perfidious cause: the crisis had not been provoked by poverty, by late flooding of the Nile, or by pestilence, as had always been the case previously, but, on the contrary, by abundance."

"By abundance," Hemiunu repeated. "In other words, by prosperity."

Cheops raised his eyebrows. An angle of twelve degrees, noted the architect-in-chief. Fifteen . . . May heaven help us!

"To begin with, it had proved extremely difficult to get a grip on this cause," he continued. "Many enlightened minds, many men trusted by the Pharaoh, who had been the first to explain it, were rewarded for their discovery by death or deportation. But the explanation they had given for the crisis—that prosperity, by making people more independent and freer in their minds, also made them more resistant to authority in general and to the power of the Pharaoh in particular—slowly overcame all the objections that had been raised at the start and gradually imposed itself. Day by day, everyone came to share the view that this crisis was more serious than any of those that had preceded it. A single question remained to be answered: How would the solution be found?

"The Pharaoh sent the astrologer-magician Sobekhotep into the Sahara to meditate on the problem in total solitude. Forty days later he returned disfigured, as happened in fact to most people who went to commune with the desert so as to bring back its message. It was more fearful than might have been expected: what had to be done was to eliminate prosperity.

"The Pharaoh, and in his wake the whole palace, plunged into deep thought. Destroy prosperity? But how? Floods, earthquakes, a temporary drying-up of the Nile, such ideas crossed all their minds, but not one of them was within their power. War? That was a double-edged weapon, and could rebound, especially given the circumstances they found themselves in. So what could be done? To do nothing at all in the face of a threat of that kind was simply not possible. One way or another, they would have to listen to the voice of the desert, or else they risked falling headlong into disaster.

"Rumor had it that it was Reneferef, the guardian of the harem, who bizarrely suggested looking for some mechanism that would sterilize part of Egypt's riches. Ambassadors serving in the lands of the Orient reported huge waterworks in Mesopotamia, on a scale out of all proportion, people said, to their economic product. If that was so, and it probably was so, then Egypt also needed to find some means of consuming the excess energy of its population. To launch works colossal beyond imagining, the better to debilitate its inhabitants, to suck them dry. In a word, something exhausting, something that would destroy body and soul, and without any possible utility. Or to put it more precisely, a project as useless to its subjects as it would be indispensable to the State.

"The Pharaoh's ministers came up with many different ideas at that time: a bottomless pit to be dug in the earth, toward the gates of hell; a rampart around the whole of Egypt; an artificial waterfall . . . But though they were all inspired by elevated, patriotic, or mystical ideas, they were all rejected by the Pharaoh. The wall would come to an end one day or another, and the hole in the ground, because it was bottomless, would exasperate the people. What had to be found was something else, something that would keep folk busy night and day so that they became oblivious. But it had to be a project that could in principle be completed, without ever reaching completion. In a nutshell, a permanently self-renewing project. And one that would be really visible.

"That is how the sovereign and his ministers, as the papyri attest, slowly came to the idea of a great funerary monument. A master tomb.

"The Pharaoh was fascinated by the idea. Egypt's main edifice would thus not be a temple or a royal palace, but a tomb. Progressively Egypt would identify itself with it, and it would become identified with Egypt.

"Geometers submitted various sketches of different shapes before finally fixing on the pyramid.

"A pyramid had all the required features. It was based on an utterly sublime idea: the Pharaoh and death, or more precisely his rise to heaven. It was visible, indeed could be seen from far away. The third and conclusive argument in its favor: it was by its nature both finite and infinite. Each Pharaoh would have his own pyramid, so that even before a generation had recovered from the fatigue and stupor of construction, a new Pharaoh, with his own pyramid to build, would subjugate the people afresh. And so on, inexorably, to the end of time . . ."

The High Priest Hemiunu paused at greater length than before.

"And so, my Pharaoh," he began again, "a pyramid, before serving the afterworld, has a function in this world. In other words, before being conceived for the soul, it is conceived for the body."

He fell silent again, then drew breath before speaking at a slower pace.

"In the first place, Majesty, a pyramid is power. It is repression, force, and wealth. But it is just as much domination of the rabble; the narrowing of its mind; the weakening of its will; monotony; and waste. O my Pharaoh, it is your most reliable guardian. Your secret police. Your army. Your fleet. Your harem. The higher it is, the tinier your subjects will seem. And the smaller your subjects, the more you rise, O Majesty, to your full height."

Hemiunu spoke ever more softly, but such was his inner conviction that as his voice fell his words grew more distinct and threatening.

"The pyramid is the pillar that holds power aloft. If it wavers, everything collapses."

He made a mysterious gesture with his hands, and his eyes went blank as if they really had looked upon a field of ruins.

"So do not think, my Pharaoh, of changing tradition . . . You would fall and drag us down with you."

Hemiunu made a different gesture and closed his eyes in such a way as to indicate that he had finished speaking.

The others said much the same thing in the same funereal tone. One of them again mentioned the canals of Mesopotamia, without which the Akkado-Sumerian kingdom would long since have fallen into tatters. Another added that the pyramid was also the country's long-term memory. One day, with time, everything else would fade away. Papyri and everyday things would age, wars, famines, epidemics, the late flooding of the Nile, alliances, decrees, palace scandals, would all be forgotten, and the haughty pyramid alone, the pyramid that no force, no length of time could ever bury, or damage, or decompose, would rise up in the desert, like unto itself, until the end of time. "It has been thus, Majesty, and so it must always be thus. Nor is its shape an arbitrary one. It is a divine shape inspired in ancient geometers by Providence herself. You are in it in all its parts, at the vertex, the summit, the peak, but also in every one of the nameless blocks of stone supporting you, stuck fast against each other, shoulder to shoulder, O Majesty."

Every time that they mentioned the visible form of the work, they alluded once again to the possibility of a general collapse. Cheops then recalled the autumn morning when he had believed that his courtiers' consternation over this pyramid business had been only a symptom of their servility. Now he saw the extent of his mistake. Their distress had been quite genuine. He was henceforth convinced that the pyramid would not just be his own, but equally, if not more, theirs.

He raised his right hand to let them know that he wished to bring the audience to an end.

With their hearts in their mouths, they listened for the Pharaoh's brief, dry, and sober judgment:

"Let the pyramid be built. The highest of all. The most majestic."

II

Start of Works

Quite Unlike the Preparations
for Any Other Building Site

NEWS of the pyramid's construction spread with amazing
speed, for which two explanations were offered: the
people's joy after long waiting for such tidings; or, on the
contrary, the dismay felt when a much-feared misfortune
that people hoped never to see happen finally rises over the
horizon.

Ahead of its announcement by public criers, the news had
already reached the thirty-eight different provinces of the
kingdom, had spread everywhere, like sand blown by yesterday's wind of disquiet.

"The Pharaoh Cheops, our sun, has decided to grant the
people of Egypt a grandiose and sacred mission, the most
majestic of all buildings and the most sacred of all tasks, the
construction of his pyramid."

The drum rolls echoed from village to village, and even

before the voices of the heralds had died away, provincial dignitaries put their heads together to deliberate on steps to be taken on their own initiative before instructions reached them from the capital. Their faces seemed lit with joy as they left the square for their homes, repeating, At last, as we had foreseen, the great day has come! From that day on there was something new in their stride, in their gestures, in the way they held their heads. A kind of hidden exultation tended to contract their muscles and to tighten their fists. The pyramid entered their existence so readily that in barely a few days they began to mutter, How the devil did we manage without it up to now?

Meanwhile, without waiting for the arrival of directives from the center, they acted as their predecessors had acted for all previous pyramids: they stifled the voices of the malcontents. The mere idea that thousands of people, instead of rejoicing at the news, could wail despairingly, "Woe! Another round!" put them beside themselves with anger.

"Did you think you were going get away with it? Did you believe that everything had changed, that there would be no more pyramids and that you could live as you liked? Well now, you see how things are! So bow your heads, and grouse to your heart's content!"

In the capital the situation had become perceptibly more tense. Not only the mien and bearing of the functionaries but the buildings themselves seemed to have grown stiffer. Coaches shuttled between the White House, as the Finance Building was called, and the Pharaoh's palace, between the palace and the building that was said to house the secret service, and even to unknown destinations, toward the desert.

Architects in the leading group directed by Hemiunu worked overtime. The plan seemed ever more complex to them, and each of them imagined that, when he finally managed to comprehend it in its entirety, his brain would burst from the pressure. What contributed above all to the mental torture was that everything hung together. A minor correction to the height or the base dimension led to an infinite number of other changes. Items that were apparently distinct from the overall plan—the decoy galleries, the air vents, the sliding doors that gave onto nothing, the secret entrances that unfortunately led to blank walls, the false escape routes, the pressure on the gallery that led to the funereal chamber, the gradient, the sinkholes, the axis, the number of stones, the horror of the center, not one of these things could be conceived in isolation. The famous phrase of the father of the pyramids, Imhotep, "The Pyramid is One" (Hemiunu had reminded them of it at their first meeting), remained lodged in their minds like a driven wedge.

Each time they recalled it, Imhotep's pronouncement seemed ever more appropriate, but instead of feeling relief, they were ever more dejected. It was a truth that bared itself progressively day by day, revealing itself, in all its blinding obviousness, as a curse falling upon them.

The pyramid could only be what it was, that is to say, total. If one corner were imperfect, it would crack or begin to subside somewhere else. So, whether in suffering or in joy, you could only dwell in it by becoming part of the whole.

They now felt that the pyramid had broken free of their calculations. When they first heard it described as "divine," they had difficulty in hiding their smiles. However, they were now convinced that it concealed some other mystery. They were obsessed with the worry that the mystery might be "the secret of the center," they lost sleep over it, they wore a gloomy countenance, but, in their heart of hearts, they took pride in the extreme complication of their fate, until, one day, something unheard of occurred: though the pyramid only existed on papyrus and not a single stone had been cut for it nor even the quarries selected, yet the Theban whip factories, without waiting for orders from the State, had already doubled their rate of production!

As chariots heavily laden with their heaps of whips slowly approached the gates of Memphis, people expected the factory owners to be punished for spreading panic. But not a bit: as people soon learned, the owners received not a punishment but a letter from the highest authorities congratulating them on their foresight and their understanding of current needs.

The architects in the leading group grew even more downcast. The idea that the pyramid could have been conceived outside of their circle, and even before their drawings were complete, was a terrible blow.

Meanwhile, foreign ambassadors, feigning indifference, had communicated the news to their capitals, each in his own way. They changed their ciphers each season, so that the spies disguised as customs officials found it hard to discern whether the vases full of garlic, the stuffed sparrow hawks, or the singlets embroidered with forks and tridents that the Phoenician ambassador was allegedly sending to his mistress in Byblos were effectively vases, garlic bulbs, and women's underwear, or just the puzzle pieces of some coded report.

Only one of the ambassadors, the emissary from the land

of the Canaanites, continued to send his messages in the ancient manner, in signs carved on stone tablets. The others, and especially those from Crete and Libya, and more recently the Trojan ambassador, used ever more diabolical devices. The envoys from the Greek and Illyrian peoples who had just settled in large numbers in the Pelasgian lands were still too backward to have a clear idea of what a report, not to mention a secret report, should be; they found all these devices bewildering, had a permanent headache from them, and sighed, What misfortune it is to be so ignorant!

The one most hated by the secret police was, as always, the Sumerian ambassador Suppiluliuma. Not long before, a system of evil signs had been discovered in his country that was called "writing." Almost indistinguishable lines and dots were traced on clay tablets, looking like the marks of crows' feet; apparently these lines and dots had the power to mummify the thoughts of men, just as bodies could be embalmed. And as if that were not quite enough, these tablets were baked in ovens and then sent from one to another as messages. You can imagine what happens in their capital, the Egyptian ambassador gloated when home on leave. All day long chariots full of clay tablets trundle around from one office to another. A letter or a report takes two or three chariots. Street porters unload them, and when perchance a tablet is broken, then there's a riot! Then other men carry the message to the minister's office. A whole half-day of unloading in dust and muddle. Upon my word, the country is off its rockers!

The things that could be heard said in the Foreign Ministry reached such a pitch that Cheops himself had to rebuke his officials. Instead of grinning at their neighbors, they would be better employed deciphering the meanings of these signs.

From that day on a policeman was on duty outside the Sumerian embassy. Barely did the spy see wisps of smoke rising above the building than he ran to give the alarm: A report! Among the secret policemen there was no doubt that the message had something to do with the pyramid; but when they thought that these devilish signs had nothing to do with sacrosanct Egyptian hieroglyphs, then their exasperation stuck in their gullets. The Canaanite ambassador, on the other hand, deserved to be kissed on the forehead. He was a bit of a plodder, to be sure, like all those desert people, but he did not lower himself to such madness. He hammered on stone, bang-bang, like an idiot, all week long, he could be heard as far away as the Foreign Ministry, but he did not demean himself with garlic, women's panties, or oven-baked clay.

It was henceforth obvious that news of the pyramid's construction had spread faster than could easily be imagined, not only throughout the two Egypts but also in neighboring lands. The event was judged to be of universal importance, and the first reports from Egyptian plenipotentiaries revealed that the information had everywhere caused great excitement. Cheops himself read and reread these messages many times over. What had surprised him at first, namely the approval of the pyramid plan by Egypt's very enemies, now seemed, after the explanations given him by Hemiunu and especially by Djedi the magician, perfectly logical. To be sure, Egypt was disliked, and the weakening of the State would be welcomed; nonetheless, an Egypt without pyramids, an *apyramidal* kingdom (as Egypt's enemies called it among themselves) would have struck them, at all events, as even more redoubtable. They feared that a slackening of the State, possibly followed by a rebellion, might have repercussions for them, as had occurred seventy years earlier, when, before they could rejoice at the weakening of the Pharaoh, the hurricane that had swept their neighbor away had almost carried them off as well.

The magician was of the view that, instead of subscribing to the arguments of the senile functionaries in the Foreign Ministry, Cheops should cease to disparage the canals of Mesopotamia. Despite being made of water and not at all imposing, he insisted, they were of the same essence as Egyptian stone. Digging them required no less suffering than the building of solid monuments. The exhaustion and stupor that they engendered were of the same order.

Other reports revealed that everywhere in Egypt people were talking only of the pyramid and that each individual and each event was systematically thought of in its relation to the great work. Some women remained indifferent to these rumors, believing they were not concerned, until one fine morning they discovered that their husband, their lover, or all their children of school age bar none had to leave for the Abusir quarries—and then you heard tears, or shouts of joy.

It was becoming ever clearer that the claim that it would take a good ten years to build the roads needed for the construction of the pyramid had a double meaning. In fact, the construction of the access routes, above and beyond the actual work, also involved preparing people for the great work, eliminating all their uncertainties, and, above all, bringing them to renounce their previous way of life. And it would be just as hard to arouse enthusiasm and to overcome lassitude, slander, and sabotage.

All were now quite convinced that despite the absence of any trace of the dust that normally accompanies building work, the pyramid had germinated and already grown strong roots. As elusive as a chimera, its premature ghost stalked the land and weighed on the spirit as oppressively as any block of masonry. The pyramid had sent its ghost as a sign, as did all great events, and there were many who impatiently awaited the start of the works in order to escape from this nightmarish apparition.

The leading group of architects now knew that thousands of people who had never drawn the merest sketch were thinking of the pyramid in the same feverish state as they were. After supper, at friends' houses, they no longer felt quite so proud, nor were they as much the center of everyone's attention as they had been. "What's the pressure of masonry you keep on about?" a young painter asked one day of one of the architects, at a little birthday reception. "If you knew what pressure I feel in my stomach . . . A thousand times harder to bear than the one you alluded to . . ." "But it's the same one!" someone else interjected. "Don't you understand? It's the same weight!"

As if to trace out the pyramid's invisible plumb lines, inspectors had set off for the four corners of Egypt. Quarries had to be selected before routes could be laid down for the stone to reach the construction site. Fast horse-drawn coaches left Memphis before dawn. Some traveled toward the old seams of Saqqara and Abusir, others to the Sinai desert, where basalt and malachite were to be found. But most of them hastened toward the south, where the most famous quarries were situated. They stopped at Illak and El Bersheh, carried on along the royal road toward Harnoub and Karnak, branched east in the direction of Thebes and Hermonthis, wheeled back toward the west to get to Luxor, then went on down like the wind, skirting Aswan, and, white with dust, rushed headlong, as if they were seeking the world's end, far, far away, to Gebel Barkal, and farther still, toward the banks of the fifth cataract, to the hamlet that was reputed to be the gateway of hell.

Cheops's orders were categorical: nothing was to be spared for his pyramid, and the stones and basalt were to be brought, if necessary, from the farthest regions.

Day by day the quarry map acquired a great variety of new symbols. All quarries were marked on it: old ones sung by poets in hymns comparing them to mothers, but now barren; disused ones that could be reopened; undug ones that still aroused the inspectors' imagination. In conversation, and sometimes in their notes and on their maps, they designated these different sites with words and expressions of a feminine kind. As their tours of duty lengthened, so their longing for the body of a woman and the intensity of their desires increased. It was sometimes even reflected in their reports: a quarry would be described as fertile, chubby, well-rounded—or, on the contrary, as sterile, or as having aborted twice already. To such an extent that, had they not first been corrected by the eunuch Toutou, Cheops might have concluded that the reports came to him not from a squad of inspectors but direct from the fleshpots of Luxor.

Cheops kept a close eye on the progress of the operation. Once a week he would visit the room in the palace that had been set aside for the main architects. On the walls there were dozens of papyri bearing all sorts of signs, arrows, and calculations that Hemiunu explained to him in a whisper.

The Pharaoh did not breathe a word; everyone had the impression that he was in a hurry for one thing only: to leave.

On one occasion, however, on the day when the model was first exhibited, he did stay a little longer. His eyes filled with a cold gleam. This smooth object of soft limestone presented its white silhouette, while the pyramid itself was still scattered and disseminated throughout Egypt. It was yet but a breath, a ghost, a black haze that would expand to infinite size like the death-rattle of a djinn. Would they manage to contain it, or would it, like a vapor, escape their grasp?

Cheops had a headache. He was worried. Something kept on slipping his mind, returning, then evaporating once more. He could not grasp the exact relationship of that stubby piece of chalk to the pyramid that only existed in anyone's mind in the state of a vapor, and especially with the third pyramid, the real one, the one that remained to be built. Sometimes the first seemed to him to be sliding between the other two, sometimes it seemed to be darting around in front and behind them like a dybbuk.

Hemiunu went on talking to him. He explained why he had chosen a slope of fifty-two degrees rather than one of forty-five. He invoked the legendary name of Imhotep, the first pyramid builder, provided information about the new pyramid's orientation, which had been fixed by the position of the stars, but Cheops's mind was elsewhere. He got a better grip on himself when the High Priest used a piece of a plank to show on the model how the stones would be raised. "That's just what I wanted to ask," said Cheops. "At such heights . . ." "No problem, Majesty," the architect replied. "You see this wooden scaffolding? We shall build four like that, one for each slope. The stones and the granite blocks that serve to obstruct the entrances will all be hauled up the ramp by means of ropes."

He propped the piece of wood against the model. It would lean on the pyramid, like that, there you are. On the lower steps the gradient of the ramp would be very gentle. Then as the height increased the slope would get steeper, which would make it harder to raise the stones. To keep it manageable, in other words to keep the angle of slope at less than twelve degrees, the ramp would be progressively extended in length. That's how, like this . . .

The architect removed the first ramp and put a second, longer one in place. "You see, Majesty, this one reaches the pyramid at mid-height, but the gradient is just about the same." Cheops nodded his head to indicate that he had understood. "And so we shall go on, to the summit," the architect continued, moving into place a third and much longer piece of wood. "Now the pyramid looks like a comet," Cheops said, and for the first time he smiled.

Hemiunu sighed with relief. "And what's that arrow, there?" the Pharaoh asked, pointing the rod he held in his hand toward a sign.

For a short interval the architect held his tongue.

"That is the gallery that leads to the funeral chamber, Majesty," he replied without looking at Cheops.

The Pharaoh touched the sign with the tip of his rod.

"And where is the chamber itself?"

"It has not been included in the model, Majesty. It has no place in it, because it is situated outside of the pyramid. It is buried underground. One hundred feet deep, maybe more . . . At a point where the weight of the pyramid is no longer felt . . ."

Cheops's eyes wandered for a moment to the abyss where they planned to place his coffin. He recalled a dream he had had a few days before. He had seen his own mummy floating in the void like the body of a drowned man.

"That is how the great Zoser and the unforgettable Seneferu, your father, were placed," said Hemiunu, lowering his voice.

Cheops did not reply. He hardly felt at his ease, but made an effort not to let it show. Only the rod in his hand trembled.

"Such matters are your business," he blurted out in the end, and then turned on his heels. His last words: "Start your work," which he uttered once he had crossed the threshold and without turning his head, reached the architects as if enveloped in an echo: Sta-start you-your wo-work!

Those left behind kept quiet for a moment, like the followers of a sect who had seen some miracle. Approval had finally been granted. The model, the seed of the future pyramid, which only yesterday they had handled and treated without ceremony, now seemed untouchable. Its cold chalky lightness seemed to needle them, and not just them, but the whole world.

The access roads were built according to the rules, that is to say simultaneously from different points in the kingdom. All trace of the old routes leading to the previous pyramids had disappeared a long time ago. Here and there, you could make out barely a few remnants, the scars of wounds healed years before. But even if they had survived they would not have been easy to use for the new pyramid. Each one had its own routes, which depended in some cases on the state of the old quarries and on the new quarries that had to be opened, on the kind of granite used (whether it was Aswan or Harnoub stone), on the choice of alabaster or basalt for interior decoration or for the summit, called the pyramidion, as well as on the material from which the sarcophagus would be carved—hard rock, red granite, or basalt. The other materials that would be brought to the site ready-made—the granite buffers for blocking the entrances, the pedestals and plaques that would bear the inscriptions—could of course be conveyed along the old roads, but sometimes also needed new ones. Everything depended on the place where they were manufactured.

All that no doubt made up the most precious and elaborate part of the project, but the main thing was the stones. Dozens of high officials in charge of works lost sleep over their extraction and haulage. As if it was not enough to have to devote most of their energies to these myriad nameless lumps, they were obliged in addition to spend days and nights on drafts and endless calculations of all kinds.

It was not just a matter of determining the exact number of stones needed, nor the average number of man-hours required for the extraction and loading of each block. After loading came haulage, and that was where everything went awry. Since it was indispensable to use the Nile for moving masonry and other materials, all their plans had to take account of the water level and of the possibility of spates. In earlier times, for reasons of security, people had tried to do without the Nile, but calculations had shown that recourse to other means of movement would have doubled, not to say tripled, the length of the journeys, so that (keep your voice down!) the Pharaoh risked dying before his pyramid was finished.

In this as in all else, the Nile turned out to be irreplaceable. However, it was not at all easy to predict exactly how far rafts laden with stone or granite could travel in this or that season. You had to consider all the possibilities, especially when planning long journeys beginning as far away as Elephantine, or even further, from Dogola or Gebel Barkal.

Deep in their calculations, the high officials and the shippers entrusted with the transportation of building materials considered justifiably that the main responsibility for the pyramid lay with them; and if someone had pointed out to them that at the same time other guilds were also losing sleep over the plans for the pyramid—for example, the architects, who had not yet solved some of the problems, such as the pyramid's gradient and its orientation with respect to the stars, or the team in charge of interior arrangements, or the team of sculptors—they would certainly have retorted sourly, but those are just girlish tasks, hair-splitting fancywork! The pyramid is where dust gets under your skin, where heat and death bear down on you at every step. But the architects themselves would have snarled at the shippers in the same way, especially those who pored over their drawings of the galleries, doors, and secret passages, or busied themselves with the mysterious inner chambers, forgetting entirely that at the same time the haulers were covering half of Egypt with dust: a common porter's job!

Perhaps the very nature of each guild's task led it to think that it was the main one. That was the case for the architects, for instance, who strove to fix the right orientation for the pyramid, and for whom the local expression "to make night into a new day" had much more than a symbolic meaning. In practice, they did a good part of their work at night, when they would go to the plateau on which the pyramid was to be built, not without casting rather disdainful glances on the trench-digging team. Although it had been decided irrevocably that in order to avoid all possibility of error the monument would be oriented in relation to a fixed star, a star from the Great Bear (but absolutely not the polestar), they continued to go almost every evening to the site at the hour when the workmen were laying down their tools. Ah, the workers thought, to have business with the stars, that's what you call keeping your hands clean! Those chaps don't know what calumny and betrayal are! But just try getting this right (and they stamped the ground with their heels) at the final inspection. You can be just a couple of fingers higher or lower than the level prescribed, and your head's on the block!

As for risking your life for the slightest error, there was another group that had even more reason to fear it: the team working on the interior arrangements of the pyramid, particularly the secret entrances and exits, the device for hermetically sealing the funeral chamber, and the false entrances intended to mislead grave robbers. Ever since the time of the first pyramids, no one was unaware that the members of this group would not grow long in the tooth. All sorts of pretexts were found for convicting and suppressing them, but the real reason for such measures was well known: to bury the secrets with their inventors.

The mystery surrounding the work done by the men belonging to the magician Moremheb in collaboration with the astrologers was even thicker. They dealt with something

27

that no one knew, perhaps not even they, if you asked them point-blank, and, what was more, something that no one could even imagine. Rumor had it that it was to do with numbers that, taken together with the pyramid's orientation, celestial signs, and other temporal coordinates, could reveal the secret and incommunicable message that the pyramid would contain until the end of time.

The only team that seemed to be working without danger was the one concerned with the little pyramid, the satellite pyramid, for the Pharaoh's *kâ,* that is to say, his double. Without a coffin or funeral chamber, it required no secret entrances or exits, so that its construction team, unburdened by mysteries, could work without worry. But things were like that only at the beginning. The satellite team soon discovered that the jealousy it engendered was just as harmful, if not even more dangerous, than the menace that secrets carried with them; and so little by little those workers too became just as grumpy as the others.

It goes without saying that those who wore the gloomiest countenance were the members of the central group led by Hemiunu. Messengers came and went night and day through the great vermilion-painted gates. Those arriving were covered in dust, but those leaving were darker still. Every day something new happened, and a good half of what happened had some connection with the pyramid. Its shape was embroidered on young people's clothes, old men clipped their beards to pyramid points, and who knows how far things would have gone—had the whores of Luxor not taken them just too far by decorating their underwear with a triangle that suggested, even more than a pyramid, the delta of their pubic hair.

They were arrested one evening and taken to the police station, shouting: "Long live the pyramid! Long live whores!" Meanwhile their pimps, together with hoodlums from the rough quarters, put the commotion to use by ransacking the town center stalls.

Such facts were talked about in bars; in private homes, after dinner, they were fearfully deplored. There was talk of numerous functionaries being sent to the remoter regions. According to some rumors, it was not just people being sent to work in the quarries and basalt mines: undesirables were being removed from the city. Pure and simple deportation, people muttered, but, obviously, no one dared to call a spade a spade.

Conversation then turned again to the quarries in the south of the country, to the latest speech by the Treasury vizier, who had mentioned four times over the words "sacrifices" and "economic constraints," before coming back to the duration of the works, which would be longer than expected. At least fifteen years . . . "God, but that's almost a whole existence! And you mean to say they haven't yet begun?"

Indeed, the pyramid gave no sign of life. It seemed that the more people talked of it, the further it receded. The time came when people thought that the monument would not be built at all and that everything connected with it was just hot air and empty rumor.

At other times it was as if the pyramid was planted in the ground and no one knew when it would germinate. The torment it caused was so great that people were tempted to think that the earth itself was in pain, that it would not stop moaning, and risked being shattered by some tremor if it did not give birth to the pyramid at its term.

III

Conspiracy

ON THE construction site at Gîza, not far from the capital, the dust clouds grew ever thicker. Crowds gaped at the whirling haze as if they expected a solid shape to emerge from it. But at sundown, after work had halted and the dust had settled, the terrain that was being leveled (the sacred undersquare, as the poets called it) looked the same as before—like any piece of wasteland.

Meanwhile, everywhere else, in temples and at public gatherings, things were said to be going swimmingly. During a meeting with ambassadors, Hemiunu in person declared that construction would start very soon, maybe even before the floods. Apparently the only people to have kept clear minds in the reigning confusion were the members of the architect-in-chief's team. Just as others could see a shadow that escaped the eyes of mere mortals, so they were able to discern the outline of a monument in that nebulous blur.

However, while the inhabitants of the capital were expecting a sign that would be the pyramid's first harbinger, something quite different suddenly emerged from the powdery dust.

A very vague rumor ran round one evening. At dawn official carriages dashed through the streets of Memphis with unusual commotion. Temples stayed closed all morning. In the afternoon, the fearful rumor was on everybody's lips: a conspiracy.

All at once, the city was virtually paralyzed. News that the Akkado-Sumerian army was at the gates of Memphis, or that the Nile had taken offense and abandoned Egypt, would hardly have caused a greater stir.

The main thoroughfares of the capital were deserted before nightfall. People were still scurrying about the backstreets, pretending not to know each other, or else actually failing to recognize each other. Whorls of smoke rose from the chimneys of the Sumerian embassy. The spy on watch cried out: A report! and ran like a hare to the police station.

News of the plot spread like wildfire.

It had all begun by chance, like most great disasters, from an apparently innocuous event: a block of basalt that had been forgotten—quite fortuitously, it appeared—in the desert of Saqqara. But it was the night of the full moon, and the basalt emitted a terrifying glow in an evil direction. As it was later discovered, all that had been planned. The block was intended to receive and then be in a position to transmit nefarious rays so that, once in the pyramid, it would draw an ill fate upon it.

Suspicion fell immediately on the magician Horemheb, but while he was waiting to be arrested, the vizier of the warehouses, Sahathor, was put in chains. However, that was just the beginning. The authorities flung into jail, in turn, two counselors, Hotep and Didoumesiou, then, for good measure, the man who was on the face of it the least likely to have been involved in this affair, Reneferef, the guardian of the harem. Moreover, it was only after the arrest of the ministers Antef and Mineptah that it became clear that the affair was not just a matter of a clutch of saboteurs, but a veritable conspiracy against the State.

The entire country trembled in terror. Cheops was dissatisfied with the results of the investigation and demanded that the plot's full ramifications be brought to light, to their furthest extent. Inspectors and spies were dispatched throughout Egypt and even abroad, especially to the enemy kingdom of Sumer, with which the conspirators were suspected of parleying.

For a fairly long while it seemed as if every other preoccupation had been forgotten, for the plot alone absorbed everyone's mind. Some opinions went so far as to stress that all the rumors about the pyramid had only been feints, a kind of trap or bluff, as people said nowadays. In fact, Cheops was still young and had no intention of having any pyramid whatsoever built so soon, and the purpose of these tall stories was quite different: they had been a way of rooting out the conspiracy.

"Are you are in your right mind, numskull, are you mad, or only pretending? What about all these stones being placed, the road that's being built, all that money and that labor? All that, you say, is just bluff?"

"Yes, bluff, and worse still, upon my word! You're the one who's lost his wits, not I. Think a bit and remember: everyone shouted from the rooftops that a pyramid was to built, but where do we see this pyramid? Nowhere! So you think that's all just by chance? Well, listen to me, you old dimwit. If the pyramid has not yet begun to rise from the ground, that's because no one is bothering about it any longer. They may all be shouting *pyramid,* but in their minds they are thinking *plot!*"

Those were the rumors that were going about before Cheops decided to make a speech. Even if it means turning Egypt upside down, he declared, I shall uncover every last root of this conspiracy!

Courtrooms and torture chambers were overflowing. The first sentences had already been passed, and the quarterings and stonings had begun in public places. So you wanted to sabotage the pyramid, did you? the fanatics screamed, still not satisfied at the sight of the piles of stones beneath which the culprit was expiring. Sometimes these heaps looked much like little pyramids, which prompted various macabre jokes, especially when the last twitches of the dying man made the pebbles move.

Most people lived in anguish. Thousands expected to be arrested, while others asked to be sent to the quarries or to join the road-building gangs. Until then they had found every possible pretext for avoiding hard labor—ill health, family commitments, and so on—but now they volunteered, without a word of complaint, in the hope that down there, in those baking and desolate places, they would be forgotten. In fact it took hardly any time at all for the dust, sweat, and terror to alter their faces so profoundly that they did indeed become unrecognizable, even to the investigators.

Who can say how long this nightmare would have lasted without the intervention of Cheops himself?

"So is this pyramid going to get built or not?" is what he was reported to have said to Hemiunu one cold morning. The latter's reply was also quoted: "But interrogation is also part of the pyramid, Majesty"—though it seems that the formula was actually invented later on.

In fact in the second month of the floods (the plain was submerged beneath the blind waters of the Nile) Hemiunu assembled his team of architects once again, just as before.

The model of the pyramid was still in exactly the place where they had left it after their last meeting. It was covered in that fine coat of dust that signifies abandonment. Nonetheless, even through the grayness, it still gave off a bad light.

Hemiunu's rod wandered over it, but without the confidence of the earlier days. Nor could the others find their words easily. Something seemed to be holding them back; their minds were clouded, as after an orgy. They talked once again of the ramps to be propped against each face of the pyramid, of the means of blocking off the galleries leading to the funeral chamber, of the quarries that would provide the stone for the first four steps, but, as they did so, their mind's eyes saw a gruesome picture—the final lists of the conspirators, their plans for getting into Cheops's palace so as to poison him, and their own wailing pleas for pardon.

They shook their heads to chase away these visions, and partly succeeded, after a while. The weight bearing on the center of the pyramid, the main routes along which the stone would be transported, the false doors, the axis of the monument, all these things were tangled up with the ramifications of the plot, with the mind that was controlling it, with the stratagems intended to camouflage it, according to the suspicions that were entertained by Cheops himself.

At times they felt that they would never escape from this fog and that what they were trying to set up was less a pyramid than a form of plot.

Their minds were so battered that it was only at the end of their third meeting that Hemiunu noticed that the head of the prosecution service and his deputy were present.

The architect-in-chief thought he had at last found the reason for the team's confusion. His face went white with anger and he asked: "Hey, you! What are you looking for here?" The chief prosecutor shrugged his shoulders as if he had not understood the question. "Out!" yelled the architect. The inquisitor and his deputy walked out in dead silence.

Straight away the flood of convictions and the zealous pursuit of the investigation both slackened, and the pyramid returned to the center of attention. The ceremony for the award of a decoration to Hemiunu (corroborating the rumor that it was he who had first unraveled the plot) was the signal for a period of reduced tension and for a new leap forward.

The immediate consequence was increased speed in all sectors of work on the pyramid. Everywhere you could see feverish activity and commotion. Clouds of dust swirled over the site where workmen were busy setting up at the greatest possible speed the barracks needed for sheltering one hundred thousand men, and especially over the now level terrain to which the first stones were being delivered.

The hour for the start of building work proper was fast approaching. The dust and the heat, instead of wearying people, now seemed to stimulate them. As long as the anxiety is cleared up, they said among themselves, all the rest is bearable! And while their hearts flowed over with gratitude for their savior, the Pharaoh, they dashed about frantically, causing more confusion and raising more sand than was necessary, in the belief that by drowning themselves in hullabaloo and dirt, they would also confound evil and divert it from its path.

Their hopes were short-lived. The day before the first stone was due to be laid, a new plot was uncovered, even more dangerous than the first.

This time, to everyone's amazement, it was the High Priest Hemiunu who fell into disgrace. After him, it was the turn of Khadrihotep, the head of the secret police, and then of the vizier for foreign affairs. A tumbrel of other high officials followed in their wake. Every morning people learned with a shudder of terror the names of those arrested during the previous night. Everyone expected more raids, and now that Hemiunu himself, the untouchable Hemiunu, had fallen, the arrest of more or less anyone seemed quite natural.

For a while the relatives of those convicted for the first plot raised their heads, thinking that the fall of Hemiunu would lead to their return to favor. But they quickly grasped that nothing of the sort would ensue. During an important meeting, a spokesman for the Pharaoh explained that even if the High Priest had indeed denounced the first plot, that did not mean that the plot itself had not existed. Hemiunu had long known about the first plot but had waited for the right moment before revealing it, so as to hoodwink the Pharaoh and to direct any possible suspicion away from his own plot, which was the more sinister.

The investigation of the new affair took its course over several weeks. Often the names of those to be arrested were known in advance, which only served to increase the general state of anxiety. Curiously, alongside fear, people also felt a morbid kind of satisfaction. They were unhealthily effusive, as if their souls had become as soft as sodden shoes, and they chattered deliriously, casting anathemas on the enemies of the State in a sort of sincere intoxication whose origins they themselves were incapable of seeing, while expressing with no lesser sincerity their adoration of their sovereign and master, the Pharaoh.

Meanwhile extraordinary rumors went around about the pyramid. Some ascribed the slow rate of work and the meager results so far to the machinations of the conspirators. Others maintained that the plan itself was ill-conceived, but they hinted that it would take decades before the flaws would come to light. A third group asserted peremptorily that everything had been done wrong—the site was wrong, the drawings were wrong, the access routes and even the quarries had not been correctly selected—with the net result that the pyramid could never be completed. Appropriate measures were taken to deal with the latter, and they soon shut their mouths. No force in the world could stop the building, it was declared at a further summit meeting. The conspirators had certainly tried to hinder it, but the damage done by them was not of a scale that would jeopardize the outcome. Nothing escaped the eye of Cheops, and however diabolical the plotters might be, they would no longer dare indulge in clumsy sabotage.

After losing the last, albeit vague, hope that had renewed their spirits for a time, people returned to their posts in a state of irremediable resignation, seeking oblivion in an atmosphere that high summer and desert dust made unbreathable.

A last wave of confusion descended on the plateau. Some people whispered that the day of the inauguration of construction work proper was near. All the same, nobody was able to give any more precise details. One morning, four workmen were crucified (in human memory, no pyramid had ever been built without workmen being sentenced to death), then, suddenly, the next dawn broke to the sound of drums announcing that the great day had finally come.

Cheops attended the ceremony in person. A fair number of new ministers and dignitaries made their first appearance in public. The High Priest Rahotep, Hemiunu's successor, came at the head of the procession, his pallor making his face look even more rigid. Foreign ambassadors and other guests, lined up on either side of the platform that had been put up for the occasion, craned their necks out of curiosity, to see the Pharaoh. Another group of guests, set behind the first and separated from it by a further line of guards, swayed like reeds in the wind. They were quite far from the rostrum, made more noise than was fitting and criticized the flamboyant hair-dye used by the new ministers, or else exchanged the very latest news, most of which had to do with the pyramid. There was a rumor that the old scribe Sesostris, when he gathered from his invitation what ceremony was involved, had exclaimed: "The pyramid? You mean it's not finished yet?"

Although this remark was mentioned with pained expressions, everyone was immediately struck by it, reckoning that the old man's words were by no means entirely misdirected.

The Pyramid

At one time or another everyone had had the impression that the pyramid had already been, if not completed, then at least more than half-built. It had been on their backs, and, more profoundly, inside them, for such a long time already that they would hardly have been surprised if someone on the rostrum that day were to declare that the pyramid whose construction was about to commence before their eyes was not the pyramid itself, but its double, or its replica.

IV

Daily Chronicle

Right-hand Face, Western Arris

THE ELEVEN thousand three hundred and seventy-fourth stone was laid during the second moon after the eclipse. It took a little more time to install than the previous one but caused fewer deaths. As if it had nothing more urgent to do than to fulfill the quota of corpses spared by its predecessor, the eleven thousand three hundred and seventy-fifth stone wrought havoc among its carriers. That is how the stonemasons Mumba, Ru, and Thutse fell, along with nine other nameless workmen; Astix the Cretan was struck down by apoplexy; and when the stone slipped back without warning, all the Libyans in the crew, as well as the Tur-Tur brothers, fourteen people in all, were squashed to pulp. Even when the stone was firmly in place and the series of deaths seemed to have come to an end, the deputy foreman died, followed by three Nubian sculptors. They had laid down on the masonry to rest a little, and it was only realized that they had stopped breathing when the supervisor came up with his whip to punish them for taking too long a break. The eleven thousand three hundred and seventy-sixth stone, despite the often unfulfilled hope of a decrease in mortality straight after a hecatomb, was just as bloody as the previous one, and dispatched just as many souls into the next world. The eleven thousand three hundred and seventy-seventh stone turned out to be less fierce and caused no more deaths than can be counted on the fingers of a hand or the toes of a foot. The three following stones could be considered to have kept their mortality rates within reasonable limits. Nothing note-worthy occurred apart from the sacking of the foreman, Unas. He was transferred to the quarry because he had allowed the legs of the two sculptors trapped during the final adjustment of the stone to stay where they had been amputated. Apart from this, the number of deaths was within forecast, and the causes were of the kind that normally cut life short. As for the crushed legs of the two unfortunate sculptors (their lifeless bodies were soon forgotten underground), long hooks were used to scrape them out in shreds when the stone was raised a little, with great difficulty. The newly appointed foreman overseeing this work explained to his crew that if human limbs were left stuck between two stones, then there was a risk that, as they decomposed, they would create a void likely to cause subsidence that, however minute, would be absolutely inadmissible in the majestic architecture of the pyramid. The eleven thousand three hundred and eighty-first stone to be raised gave off a pestilential miasma. People said that the workers at the far-distant quarry whence it came had infected it with their disease. And that must have been true, because whoever touched the stone came out in a rash of foul pustules. The eleven thousand three hundred and eighty-second stone was eagerly awaited in the hope that when placed up against its predecessor it would contain its neighbor's harmfulness. But it was of very limited use, since the larger side of the infected stone remained exposed. Apart from the deaths that it caused in this manner, the placing of the disease-ridden stone was also accompanied by the consecutive deaths of two fair-haired Pelasgians, Teut and Bardhylis, the former from a scorpion bite, the latter from despair. A most bizarre murder was also imputed to the infected stone, that of the Sumerian Ninourtakoudouriousouri, by an unnamed slave. For some time the slave refused to reveal the motive for his crime, but one summer's night, just as it had been agreed that it would be pointless to torture him any further, he confessed. He had been prompted to murder out of jealousy for the Sumerian's name, because he, as a slave, had none. Believing that the only means of obtaining a name was to take it from another while leaving the other in an inanimate state (apparently he thought that that really was the only way of appropriating a patronym), he had done the Sumerian in and thereby sealed his own fate. In fact there had been brawls on such matters before, and trading in names was not unknown between those who had one and the unnamed, who were sometimes tormented by this insufficiency, spiritually unbalanced by it, obsessed with it to the extent of losing sleep as much as any miser haunted by his gold. Even so, things had never previously gone as far as murder, unless that had happened prior to the ten thousandth stone, or even further back. Although the sale, loan, and inheritance of names was strictly prohibited in order to avoid confusion, such practices were conducted clandestinely. The arrival of the eleven thousand three hundred and eighty-third stone blurred and then completely obliterated the memory of this murder. It was during the laying of this stone that there was an increase in cases of madness; then came an outbreak of deaths from sunstroke. That had already happened before, people recalled, during the laying of the ten thousand nine hundred and ninety-ninth stone, which would not be soon forgotten since it was one of the very few blocks to have cracked because of the exceptional heat. So a bout of dementia was first suspected when Siptah the Theban was found making sketches in the sand, seeking to guess the dimensions of the work in progress, but it turned out to be nothing of the kind, to the poor man's great misfortune. He had his bones broken with millstones, a fate normally reserved for people who asked inappropriate questions. The eleven thousand three hundred and eighty-fourth stone was still far away in the baking desert when a rumor of bad omen was heard about it: this stone and the six that were coming after it, all from the Abusir quarry, had been struck by the evil eye. No one could say whether it was a maleficent force in the seams from which they had been cut, or whether the evil inhered to the stones themselves. As the haulers approached (they had resigned themselves to their lot; reckoning they were lost already, they had no fear and considered each extra day of life as an unhoped-for gift) and as the stones grew nearer, general anxiety grew sharper, more suffocating, and more irremediable. People who had already seen the stones (for dozens of reasons there was always some traveler or messenger crossing the desert) said that at first sight they looked quite normal, but had very dark veins running through them, like the kind of sign that a man may have on his forehead and that makes his whole face seem sinister. In the event, as is always the case when anxious expectation is long drawn out and the awaited occurrence, when it finally happens, seems not as terrible as had been imagined, the arrival of the stones brought a degree of relief to everyone. There were deaths, to be sure, and in fact rather more than for the preceding stones, but perhaps it was the expectant anxiety rather than the actual presence of the stones that prompted the Grim Reaper to greater vigor. That was what people spread around, but no one really got to know the truth of the matter: how can you know whether the evil engendered by an object comes after it, alongside it, or, like a running dog, ahead of it? Hopes ran high that the eleven thousand three hundred and ninety-first stone would bring respite, since the series of evil-veined blocks was now finished; but it only secreted an even more unbearable atmosphere in which a great number of mostly nameless workmen died in silence, like flies. The eleven thousand three hundred and ninety-second stone (from the El Bersheh quarry) was being maneuvered into place when the chief inspector of the pyramid arrived and had the superintendent of the west face whipped in front of the whole workforce. This corporal punishment, which prematurely hastened the superintendent's way to the other world, was justified, so people said, by the slow progress of the work. However, it was soon learned that similar punishments had been meted out on the three other faces, in the main quarries, and on the four desert roads used by the caravans that were supposed to hasten the transport and delivery of the stones, as indeed they did. But what had not been foreseen was the sinister rumor resulting from the acceleration of the building work. It was really the blackest of rumors, one of the most destructive that could be imagined. It got about that the feverish haste and impatience to complete the royal tomb only proved what the State had used every effort to hush up: that the Pharaoh was ill. A whole armory of repressive measures was therefore assembled: death sentences, strangling, torture, and even the dispatch of public criers throughout the land to deny the rumor, which, as usually happens in such circumstances, did not die down, but spread and swelled all the more. So, during the installation of the eleven thousand three hundred and ninety-third and the eleven thousand three hundred and ninety-fourth stones, both from the Elephantine quarry, a very peculiar situation developed. People did not know what to do: to expedite their work at a time when intemperate zeal could be seen as a way of supporting the rumor, or to slacken off, even though their bodies were striped with welts from whippings and other punishments meted out for just such slackness. Some said it was better to carry on working as if they knew nothing; others thought the opposite, that of the two evils, slowing down was the lesser. It seems that the majority were of the second opinion, since a wave of indolence was observed throughout the whole project: the movement of the stones through the desert slowed down by the day, as did their installation. The builders themselves became ever more languid, not just in their working movements but in their whole manner and bearing, in the way they turned their heads, or spoke, or even breathed. It was plain to see: sometimes the whole workforce looked as though it were on the point of dozing off. The eleven thousand three hundred and ninety-fifth stone and its successor would thus come to be known as the sluggards' stones. The foreman and superintendents no doubt noticed it gloomily, but none dared raise his whip to demand more application to the task, for that could easily have rebounded on them. So the mood of relative apathy continued, and, despite appearances, it concealed genuine disquiet. People discussed the pyramid more than ever before, talking of its imposing dimensions, of its shape, of the huge number of stones that it would consume. It was hard to decide whether these topics of conversation had their roots in the general chatter going round the baking-hot radius of the four great slopes, that is to say whether these topics were already known to everyone, or whether, on the contrary, they had previously been repressed in people's minds by the unbearable fatigue, by the heat and the fear of punishment, and had never previously emerged. Everyone in Egypt and far afield knew full well that tens of thousands of souls would have to spend their whole lives building a tomb, but even so an awareness of that reality had never been put in words, let alone into words strung out along one of those tunes that awake ambiguous feelings in the hearer, of the kind: "Dear mother, to say that I shall end my days building a tomb!" and so on . . . Some inquisitive minds asked: "And what will happen once the pyramid is finished?" To which another would reply: "What does it matter to you, you poor fool, what happens afterward, since you won't be there to see it!" Someone else would explain that after this pyramid they would put up another one for the Pharaoh's son, then another for his grandson, and so on, in perpetuity, until the end of time. The representation of life as an unending succession of pyramids cast most people into the deepest gloom; others, fewer in number, felt vague resentment. It was perhaps more that latter sentiment than the slowing down of the work that most aroused the foremen's and superintendents' disapproval. They had heard from their predecessors, who had it from their own predecessors, that this feeling was not new, that a similar slackening had occurred long before, prior to the seven thousandth stone, perhaps even prior to the four thousandth, and things had got so bad then that several stones had been shattered. That's what had happened, but afterward measures had been taken, mouths had been shut and minds too, things had been put back in right order, just as the stones had been put in their right and eternal places in the pyramid. Since they were convinced that the slack period would pass, the superintendents and foremen bided their time with confidence, for everything that happened around the pyramid had a cyclical nature and was thus destined to end. Another period would come, with other stones, and everything would be like before. Meanwhile, at least according to what people said, reports of the current situation had gone right up to the Pharaoh, whose reaction had been awaited but was never expressed, and in the end things were left as they were. Apparently a blind eye had been turned in order to emphasize how certain it was that the Pharaoh would live for a very long time, so that there was no need to be worried about the slow rate of the building work on his tomb. This line of reasoning had even been pushed so far that one unfortunate member of the government (so people said) had proposed, as a logical consequence, to break with tradition and to suspend work on the pyramid altogether, so as to show clearly that the Pharaoh was immortal. Daring initiatives often lead to results quite at odds with their intention, and the dignitary who thought up this bold argument paid for it with his life. He was dissected alive, beginning with the tongue that had proffered the idea, and going on to the throat, the lungs, and the hands that had participated in the speech, and so on, until more or less nothing of his body remained. This mutilation signaled an immediate about-turn. A new plot was uncovered in the capital. The first wind of fear could be smelled on the work sites long before any message or order reached them. The situation was turned around from top to bottom. A surge of tension ran around all four faces of the pyramid like a shudder and immediately made people move faster around the stones, lower their voices, and keep their eyes down to the ground. Grumbling, and conversation in general, became less frequent. And not only words, but also the ideas that prompted them, tended to dry up. That was how great droughts announced themselves: each day the winch would haul up less water, proving that the well was running dry. A dry wind blew or rather pressed on people's temples and served to clean out misleading memories. Every passing day fell deeper into oblivion, and the time of the eleven thousand three hundred and ninety-fifth and ninety-sixth stones, when there had been culpable talk, hopes, and dreams, now appeared a forbidden fruit. (Thereafter for a long period the supervisors, when whipping prisoners, would gloat: "So, you thought we'd gone back to the days of ninety-five and ninety-six? So take that! and that!") Upon which, the eleven thousand three hundred and ninety-seventh stone was delivered: heavy, unyielding, identical to the thousands and thousands of other stones that had been placed at the foot of the pyramid, this stone was the symbol of order restored, and caused a sigh of relief among the supervisors and foremen. The hours and the days merged into the hours and the days of yore, and the deaths, the scorpion stings, the outbreaks of dementia or sunstroke, and even the names of the victims were almost indistinguishable. The eleven thousand three hundred and ninety-eighth stone, from the Saqqara quarry, caused more or less the same number of deaths and mutilations as the previous stone. The day before it was hauled up into place, a snake coiled up in a ball had slept on it, but no one could say whether that should be considered a good or bad omen, since no one had any kind of perspective any more. Like its predecessors the stone was maneuvered into its place while a cloud of sand on the horizon foretold the arrival of another stone, the eleven thousand three hundred and ninety-ninth, and then came more, and so on, without relief, unto the end of the ages, O heaven!

V

The Pyramid Rises toward the Sky

CONSTRUCTION was taking longer than expected. A monstrous cloud of dust hung over the huge plateau where, day after day, several hundred thousand men scurried about like ants. It could be seen tens of miles away. In far-flung villages people who turned their heads unthinkingly toward it every morning would not have been at all surprised if they had been told that the site was partly situated in the sky.

Pyramids had been built in the past, but there was no memory of any having created such stupor and weariness. Exhaustion, the terror of execution, and the fear of being sent to the quarries were not the sole causes of despair. An ill wind blew over the whole land. Everything was awry, and good could no longer be told from evil. Some people said that Egypt was under a curse. What was more, the pyramid that was supposed to ennoble mankind had made Egyptians worse than they had ever been before.

A very few held the pyramid responsible for its own ills. A tomb of such outlandish proportions in the very middle of the country was bound to attract misfortune, they whispered. Furthermore it was an insane burial place, the grave was not at the bottom, like in any other tomb, but in the air—in a word, it was an upside-down tomb. No use at all. To be sure, Re had put up with the mastabas and the previous pyramids as much as he could, in the hope that the Egyptians would eventually put a halt to their lunatic habit and bury their dead in the ground, like all other folk, but he had finally come to the conclusion that, far from giving up their tradition, they were forever increasing the height of their graves, and so had decided to intervene.

This last feature, the height of the funerary monument, was precisely what was considered to be the root of all misfortunes by some of those who still wished the building of the pyramid to continue.

Its height was truly fearsome: three times greater than the average pyramid. Even when it was only halfway up it made people dizzy just to look at it. Imagine what they felt later on! Some people insisted that when it got to three hundred cubits, and even more, when it reached its final height of four hundred and fifty, you might well wonder what would happen!

In the temples priests tried to calm people's spirits. Their imposing voices boomed through the smoke rising from the sacrifices: "Do not heed foolish and mischievous chatter! The pyramid will make us stronger and happier! It will help heaven and earth to reach a better understanding!"

Foreign missions headed by ambassadors took turns to

visit the site. They were all struck dumb as they got out of their carriages; some knelt on the ground. The whole world's eyes were on Egypt, for what that country was achieving was the greatest wonder on earth. That was more or less the gist of the comments they made.

A delegation of Greeks from Crete, backward as they were, were the only ones who could make no sense of the building's proportions. At first sight they took the unfinished construction for a labyrinth, since their brains were unable to encompass a tomb so tall and so convoluted. It was later said that an Egyptian delegation summoned by them had paid them back in like coin, declaring that their labyrinth was no more than a disoriented pyramid.

Meanwhile some of the foreigners who were particularly well known for their devotion to Egypt were taken to temples to make speeches. They spoke of the glory of the country and of the balancing role of the pyramids. Egyptians would do well to visit their neighbors, so as to appreciate the peace and harmony that reigned at home. In these other lands it was cold, people were sad, and it never stopped raining. Moreover, earth and heaven never stopped arguing with each other. The weather was always bad, and a heavy vapor that was called fog seeped in from the other world, making you think that each dawn was the last of your life.

People came out of the temples feeling relieved. How lucky we are, they said, to have our pyramid! Otherwise the devil only knows what might become of us. The sky might suddenly get angry and flick its fire-whip at us. Not to mention that other most terrible calamity whose very name spreads panic, when the firmament plunges into deepest misery and flock, like clumps of beggar's hair, falls continuously from it, covering the land in white and making it as cold as a corpse.

This flood of flattery from foreigners did not stop diplomats from expressing rather different views in their secret reports. It had been suspected for a long time, of course, but it became quite transparent when the Sumerian ambassador's report was finally intercepted. His prolix style—for which he had been reproached more than once by his superiors, moreover—served indirectly to set the trap he fell into. While the two overloaded wagons of the diplomatic courier were conveying his message (it weighed about the same as the side of a house—despite the diplomat's efforts to have thinner tablets made, he had been unable to reduce their weight any further), the Egyptian secret service had had a hidden trench dug across the highway, and so easily got the carts to tip over. In the ensuing confusion and while the injured couriers were receiving first aid, purloining a few of the tablets scattered over the road was hardly a problem. The fragments were quite enough to prove how bitter Sumer's venom was.

It was at an official dinner over a week after deciphering had been completed that Cheops made his celebrated pronouncement: "Our enemies are exasperated at the idea of our pyramid, but the more they speak ill of it, the higher we shall raise it toward heaven!"

Those present found it difficult to hide their trembling hands. The Pharaoh grew more sullen by the day. People mentioned that a new plot had been uncovered, but nothing precise was known about it yet.

▲

The whole week long people expected the main team of architects to be arrested. They were visited in the end, not by the police, but by a palace messenger bringing an order to appear before Cheops, bringing the model with them. Rahotep, the architect-in-chief, was as white as a sheet and had to make an effort to stand up straight in front of Cheops, whose eyes ran over every detail of the object before sinking beneath it, as if he were looking for something underground. The rod he held in his hand was twitching. "I am buried too deeply, there," he blurted out at last, pointing his rod to an invisible point beneath the miniature pyramid.

The terrified architects were at first unable to make out what he was referring to, but understood in the end all the same. He meant the funeral chamber. They had often thought about it. They knew full well that Cheops had reservations about the builders' idea of placing his body underground. In fact he seemed principally concerned not to be laid to rest outside of the actual substance of the pyramid. Maybe he feared solitude. But the old archives and even the personal notes of the genius Imhotep offered no other solution.

"Don't give me any nonsense about technical problems," Cheops said. "I don't want to know about the weight of the masonry. A lot of rubbish! I want to be raised higher up inside the pyramid itself. Got that?"

"Very well, your Majesty," Imhotep replied in a voice that seemed to come from beyond the grave.

The architects departed silently with their model. Back in their studio they held their tongues for a long moment. Their minds were alternately paralyzed and convulsively agitated. Apparently that is how you begin to go mad.

They had conceived the funeral chamber as a kind of

gateway through which the pyramid would communicate with the lower depths. It was the pyramid's root, the anchor that moored it to the earth.

And now he wanted them to abandon the gateway, to raise the chamber. To stick it in between two lumps of masonry! It would be horrible. Eventually the weight of the stone would crack such a funeral chamber like an egg, and crush the sarcophagus and the mummy with it!

The architects were at a loss. As for Rahotep, he thought he had already gone mad. And it was probably that belief that saved him, and the others too. For days and nights at a stretch he thought himself into the masonry. He strove to imagine the torture and despair of being held motionless in the dark. Sometimes he felt as if he had become aware of a new kind of distress in such irrevocable solitude. For instance, he imagined a stone shattered by the weight of surrounding masonry but, despite being in smithereens, unable to fall: it would stay where it was, unseen, its unhappy fate unknown, for all eternity.

When Imhotep came to the studio one day in a jolly mood, the other architects reckoned he really had gone mad. They were probably jealous of him, and began to hope that they too would follow him into insanity.

Rahotep had brought a number of drawings with him. The others pretended to pay attention to what he said, the way adults do with children, so as not to upset them. But suddenly in the midst of his prattle they heard him come out with something amazing. In order to reduce the weight of masonry on the funeral chamber, he said, you could construct a layered set of cavities above it, so that the pressure would bear only on the walls, and the relative distance between the funeral chamber and the vertex could be reduced by an equivalent amount.

The architects could hardly believe their ears. It was most certainly an idea of genius. Privately they blamed themselves for not having thought of it earlier. They looked on their boss with a mixture of wonderment and affection, without quite grasping what had just happened.

The next day they requested an audience with the Pharaoh. He listened to them glumly.

"Now, Majesty, you will be placed here," said Rahotep, pointing on the model to the level where the funeral chamber would be situated.

Cheops sighed deeply, which was unusual.

"Higher!" he said in a stifled voice. "I am still too low!"

"I understand, Majesty," replied the architect-in-chief.

"I want to be in the middle," Cheops declared.

"I understand, Majesty."

The whites of the Pharaoh's eyes seemed to be wrinkled with immense weariness.

The half-suspected plot was not revealed during construction of the thirteenth or the twelfth step down, after the minister Menenre had slit his wrists. But with the eleventh, you heard people say almost everywhere, it could not fail to come to light. That is to say, if there really was a plot.

During the tenth step down some squabbling broke out between the foremen on site and the inspectors who came down from the capital to check the numbering system. The foremen maintained that they had indeed got to the tenth row down, while the visitors would not budge from the view

that they were only at the twelfth, if it was not still the thirteenth. (Since counting from the base, that is to say from
ground level, had been stopped by order of the new architect-
in-chief and replaced by top-down numbering from the vertex, such muddles were only to be expected. How can you
start counting from something that isn't there? grumbled
most of the builders. It's like trying to cast an anchor in the
clouds!)

Numbering the masonry rows in reverse, counting down-
ward as the pyramid went up, made everyone feel somewhat
uneasy, gave them a disorienting sensation of void and
vertigo. People went off the wrong way, bumped into things
that they had only imagined, or else failed to notice obstacles
that were really there. It had all become so intolerable that
most of the master builders had gone back to counting in the
old way until the architect-in-chief issued a categorical
order: although the final row of the pyramid had yet to be
determined, henceforth all numbering must be done top
down; any other way of reckoning would be taken as a sign
of rebellion. A circular intended to make things crystal clear
stated that the pyramid was in its present phase increasingly drawn toward the sky so that the enhancement of its
heavenly progress was an imperious necessity that would
already have been met had it not been hampered by outdated
ideas.

"Old or new, those ideas won't change my mind," said
the master builder Hankou. "All it comes to is like working
upside down." But afterward he had to admit that there was
nothing to be done about it, that you had to bend to this
whim, that it was in the end just one more thing that was
assbackward in Egypt. ("Our whole country lives like that,

upside down and back to front. Only an overthrow of the regime, and of the Pharaoh too, could put things back to right." These statements had been reported verbatim to the investigating magistrate, who waved the papyrus under his nose and yelled: "Confess! Confess that you said that! Look here, are these not your very words? Don't you see?" "I see them," the master builder replied, even though both his eyes had been put out in the very first week of torture.)

During the seventh step a great fear seized hold of everyone, not just those working permanently on site but all whose tasks obliged them to spend a few moments near the pyramid. "What is it?" they asked in horror. "Why, what's going on?" they enquired of the Seveners, as they had begun to be called . . . "No, no, it's nothing. I must have had a hallucination, it was probably just giddiness, I have to get back up, see you soon . . ."

For a while they would watch the silhouettes hopping from step to step, growing smaller in the distance before disappearing into the dust of the human anthill. Those who were up there, above the rest, looking down on the mass, far from feeling more confident, shook like leaves. They would turn to look at the point where the vertex was going to be and were utterly petrified. They were right up against the sky, and each of them thought in his heart of hearts that it was probably this celestial proximity that made him feel quite weightless, convinced him of his own inanity, and inflicted him with such a burden of guilt.

▲

Although almost nothing happened during the building of the seventh step, the masons suffered inwardly so much that as soon as it was finished (an immediate start was then made on the sixth step down) they truly believed that they had been through martyrdom. From time to time, especially during the midday break, they recounted fragments of their nightmares to each other, in good faith, as if they were talking of things that had really happened.

Crumbs from their stories (or rather, their ravings) floated down somehow or other, falling slowly from heaven like dust (or rather, antidust) and settled on the milling crowd at the base of the site.

In the evenings when they came down to return to their barracks they could feel the eyes on their backs, full of awe and admiration. The looks seemed to say: My poor friends, those are the real heroes, what hell they must be suffering up there! They were treated as if they had come straight from heaven, and people even seemed surprised that none of them had yet made use of his nearness to the sky to step over into the other world, the way a man can jump from a roof onto the balcony next door.

The curiosity surrounding the builders of step seven was but a foretaste of the even livelier interest aroused by the vertex. Now that the pyramid's completion was imminent, everyone was obsessed by its topmost point. Some said that the hour of truth was about to strike. They feared that the pyramid was too high and that its peak would scratch or even injure the sky. "Then you'll see what has to happen! Wretched that we are! Where can we go to hide?"

But others objected: "How can we be responsible? We were just carrying out orders. If there has been a mistake, others are to blame."

"But we are all guilty," the former maintained. "In one way or another we are all involved in this nasty business."

Having said that, they raised their eyes mechanically toward the sky. It was not just the pyramid, but also their own bodies and their very fates that were being siphoned upward by the celestial void.

VI

Dust of Kings

THE SKY was overcast. Cheops paced back and forth on the upper floor of his palace, feeling tense. Though he was trying not to look anywhere at all, he could not prevent his head from turning toward the west, toward the spiraling tornadoes of dust, blacker than any seen before. It looked as if a sandstorm were brewing for the afternoon. But the pyramid's dust cloud could be seen from everywhere, running ahead of the hurricane. Cheops felt as if his own tomb were galloping across the sky like a bolting horse. The vision had not left him for years. He consoled himself with the thought that it was his fate as a monarch, that there was no one to whom he could complain, but it made him melancholic just the same.

Two sets of scrolls were laid out on a marble shelf. One was thick and weighty and contained the biography of his father Seneferu, recently completed by a team of historians.

Cheops had asked to look at it before choosing the layout of his own biography, which would soon be started. The other set of scrolls contained the current affairs of state.

He would wait for another day before unrolling his father's life: today his soul was too much like a sea of bitterness. And he almost had to do violence to himself to pause in front of the shelf. The manuscript was in two parts: the first, dealing with life on earth, was encased in red leather; the second, colored sky blue, dealt with the afterlife.

He thought that he knew more or less what the first scroll would consist of. The king's youth, his coronation as Pharaoh, first military campaigns, reforms, then alliances with neighboring states, major decrees, conspiracies unraveled, wars, hymns written by poets. But the second whetted his curiosity. He went through it slowly, and his eyes rested on one of the papyri: "The day of Seneferu. After the day, the night of Seneferu. Then again the day of Seneferu. Then the night again. After which the day. After the day, the night of Seneferu. Then after the night, another day of Seneferu. After this day, the night . . ."

Good god! he groaned. He imagined himself inside his sarcophagus, alone in the mortuary chamber. He put his own name in the place of his father's: Day of Cheops; night of Cheops . . . His dismay was so great that it stopped his anger short. That was what his posthumous biography would be like . . . The first papyrus was entitled *The First Three Hundred Years*. But if the first three hundred were as monotonous as that, there was no reason to expect any change in the following centuries.

He unrolled the scroll further. He found the same words, and, again, replaced his father's name with his own: Day of

Cheops. Night of Cheops. Day of Cheops after the night of Cheops. Another night of Cheops . . .

The idiots! he growled. They had apparently counted out the days and nights of the first three hundred years, thinking they could get away with such fiddlesome listings.

He seized the manuscript as if he were grabbing a woman by the hair before throwing her to the ground, maybe even before trampling on her, when all of a sudden, at a place where he had made a tear, a different wording caught his eye.

He tore out the passage and was so surprised that his anger subsided at once. An event! he almost shouted out loud. In this uninhabited void an event, rarer than an oasis in the desert, had sprung forth. He drank in the hieroglyphs with ardor: "In the morning the highest dignitaries of the state arrived in turn. Then the High Priest of Egypt, all the ministers, and last of all the Queen presented their congratulations to the Pharaoh. At the end of the ceremony, the dignitaries having retired, he lay down in his sarcophagus. Afternoon of Seneferu. Then the afternoon of Seneferu was followed by a night of Seneferu. Then day of Seneferu." Day of Cheops . . .

He ran through the document feverishly until his eye alighted once more on an event. Significant facts were extremely rare, as if lost among a myriad of stars. Commemorations of the Pharaoh's coronation. Celebrations of his own birthdays. Some religious ceremony. So that was what his life would be in the afterworld, compared to which his present life constituted only an infinitesimal fragment. Heavens! he groaned again. These happenings were like distant posts in a desert, like the domes of temples seen on the horizon. He thought he had had a vision of this kind once before. Ah yes, it was two years previously, in a report from the security service about the philosophers of Memphis, giving a detailed reconstruction of their judgments about time. Some of them thought that time now was not what it should be, that it had lost its original quality. It had lost all restraint, it had, so to speak, gone flabby, got dilated—in a word, it had run down. According to them, real time should be very dense. For instance, the time of a human life in this world should be measured as the sum of its orgasms. All the rest was emptiness and vanity.

Cheops had only a vague memory of the arguments of the opposing faction. All he recalled was that they stood firmly by the contrary view, in other words, they defended time's need to relax. According to them, if humanity persisted in living so intensely, then it would end up losing its reason.

Gobbledygook! Cheops thought. It had been an inspired idea to send half of them off to the Abusir quarries. If people would stop bothering themselves with such nonsense then the affairs of state would run all the more smoothly. But they were incorrigible. After wracking their brains with all sorts of visions, the Egyptians were now doing their best to unhinge the rest of the world. That's what his ambassador in Crete had reported. The Foreign Minister had brought the dispatch to him, puffing with pride. The other viziers were also glowing: the Egyptians' worldwide impact was steadily increasing. Crete, and, beyond that island, the Pelasgians and the peoples who had settled there just recently, had been struck by a great confusion. They had learned from the Egyptians that another life existed, and it had quite turned their heads. We were ignoramuses, they said, we were blind, thinking life was so short and simple, whereas it is infinite!

The ambassador had reported just how excited the Cretans were. They were grateful to Egypt for a miracle that they held to be the most important discovery ever made by mankind. From now on everything would change—ideas, mentalities, even the earth's dimensions. It was no trifle, no, it was not a mere appendage or outbuilding tacked on to life. No, what had at last been brought to light was life a hundredfold, a thousandfold, not to say everlasting.

Cheops listened to his ministers in silence. To begin with, even he had not understood whence came the chill that he felt. Then when they had left he went out on the balcony of his palace and gazed for a time at the dust rising from the building site. The thought came to him, more clearly than before, that if Egypt had not made the discovery that so bedazzled the rest of the world, then there would be no pyramid either. There would be no pyramids, he thought again and again. And that horrible dust cloud would not darken his days.

Two decades previously an inner voice had advised him not to have this kind of tomb built. But his ministers had ended up convincing him of the opposite. Now, even if he had wanted, he could no longer detach himself from his pyramid.

"I did it for you!" he was about to shout out loud. "I have sacrificed myself for you!" Now they had left him alone with his pyramid, while they did nothing but banquet and carouse. Yes, he was alone before his tomb, swelling up and crouching down by turns before leaping high as if to take possession of the whole sky.

For a long while he tried to think of nothing at all. Then he felt drawn once again to the scrolls. He hoped that the sky-blue one would help to dispel his gloomy thoughts, but it was the scroll he was trying to avoid that attracted him irresistibly. He knew what was in it. But he raised its leather casing with the kind of sudden start that you use to open a door onto a group of whispering detractors.

They were there as they always were, in their insatiable thousands. From robbers and street urchins to educated ladies and lounge lizards, whose venom was all the more intolerable. Informers had faithfully copied down everything, and these unordered inventories of things said in vulgar and in polished language gave a more accurate picture by far than any report of the degree of Egyptians' loyalty to their state, and of their disaffection . . . It sucks, I swear, it sucks up everything, it ain't never satisfied, the black widow, it's left our stomachs in our sandals, it's squeezed the seeds out of us, and not just the seeds, it's all down to that thing, you can't have a laugh any more, or have fun, on my mother's soul the devil take Egypt, let me never hear its name again, not Egypt's nor the name of that bloody pyramid! . . . People are damned right to claim that the building of this new temple is impoverishing everything, even life itself. Half of the taverns have been closed since construction work began, dwellings have gotten smaller, men's love of their craft and their pleasure in entertainment have been extinguished, fear has spoiled and shriveled every kind of thing, and only one has grown: the line at the bean seller's stall. People have now realized that the pyramid not only devours everyday life, but is consuming the whole of Egypt. Its blocks of masonry have crushed the palm trees and the autumn moon, the excitement of the early evening in the city, laughter, dinner parties, and feminine sensuality . . . Even if the pyramid were to swallow it whole, Egypt should consider itself lucky to make such a sacrifice! . . . But hang on, there's no point in crying wolf! The pyramid may have petrified our existence, but one day it could also depetrify it, bring liberation, release us from the weight of its stones . . . Hell, that's just daydreaming! Have people lost their wits? Can a witch regurgitate all that she has eaten? To make her do so you have to put her to torture, cut her up into little pieces—come on, witch, spit it all up, or I'll knock up your mother too! But that's just nonsense. Supposing you did get hold of it and squeeze it hard, what would come out of it?—A huge fart and nothing more.

Cheops's jawbone hurt. For a second he felt completely empty. Then he blinked. They don't like you, he said aloud. It wasn't yet compassion that he felt. All the same, now that people were foulmouthing the pyramid, he felt less ill-disposed toward it.

He was naturally entitled to despise it. He could even detest it. But they had no right . . . no right to go so far . . .

He had fallen into the grip of some devilish tool. It was hard for him to understand what he should like and what he should abhor. Sometimes he felt as though it were he himself who bore that horrible lump on his back, yet it was the others who were complaining of it.

He felt no bitterness. He and his ugly hump stood together, together against the world.

Cheops raised his eyes. What he could see spread out against the sky was his own dust. That's what it was. The dust of kings. Alas! he sighed. Sometimes he regretted not having adopted another means of crucifying Egypt. One of those immemorial devices that his ministers had come up with from the ancient archives, about twenty years ago, on that unforgettable November morning. He could have set people to digging that great underground hole that would have been undetectable on the surface . . . Involuntarily, he often found himself thinking of how such a hole could be designed. First darkness, second darkness. On down to the fifth, the seventh darkness, the darkness of darknesses. Pitch dark. That's what the Egyptians deserved. They weren't worthy of his uprightness. They had always preferred shameless manipulation and occult oppression. Whereas his own pyramid rose up right there, in the very heart of the State, as if to say: Here I am!

They don't like you, he repeated silently. His exasperation with the pyramid had now given way to a kind of pity for it. "But I'll show them . . . I'll show them . . . No, you don't need them to like you!"

He would not force them to love the pyramid, though that would not have been very difficult. He would get his own back on them in another way. He would get them to spin out paeans of praise for the pyramid in exact proportion to their hatred of it. He would thus degrade them remorselessly, humiliate them in each other's eyes, in the eyes of their wives and children as well, and in their own consciences. He would destroy them little by little and in the end turn them into nothing more than worms.

Cheops realized he was going round in circles like a lunatic. He got a grip on himself, and though his knees had not stopped trembling with repressed rage, he managed to keep himself still. Since he had come back to the marble shelf, he naturally decided to calm down by reading the biography of his father's afterlife. But to his amazement his hands failed

to reach out for the sky-blue scroll but went instead once
again toward the other. He had heard that drunks who wake
up with a hangover ask for another cup of what had put them
in that state, because oddly enough it was the drink most
likely to clear their heads.

The word *postpyramidal*, which caught his eye in passing,
gave him the same kind of fright as the sight of a snake in
years gone by. He had expected it to return ever since he came
across it in the report before last. It hadn't been a chance occurrence . . . Another era . . . The postpyramidal period . . .

So he wasn't the only person to be racking his brains about
what would happen after the completion of the pyramid.
Others had thought about it before him seriously enough to
forge a whole new word for it.

All of a sudden Cheops saw the silver platter laden with
excised tongues that the High Priest Hemiunu had brought
to his father Seneferu one morning. At the time he was only
thirteen, and his father explained to him that the tongues
had belonged to people who had spoken ill of the State. "It
made you go pale," Seneferu remarked, "but you will do the
same one day. If you don't cut them off, in the end those
tongues will have the better of you and your reign."

But it was now probably too late for it. Wicked tongues
had proliferated to such an extent that even a thousand plat-
ters would not suffice.

He raised his head, intending to bring his perusal of the
reports to an end.

He could not take his eyes from the column of dust. He
had hated its sinister dance to the heavens, not thinking that
one day he would miss it. Even now, and in spite of his still
undiminished revulsion for it, he was already horrified to

imagine that one day it would not be there. Together he and his tomb had wielded power in concert, and now, after twenty years, the tomb was on the point of completion. Soon its infernal animation would cease. It would begin to cool day by day beneath its polished limestone facing panels before congealing forever. It would have begun by clearing out of the sky (Cheops felt almost at fault now for having sworn at all that dust) and then after taking leave of the sky it would take leave of life.

Cheops took in a sharp and painful breath. So the pyramid will leave me alone and abandoned in this vale of tears . . . An ice-cold stiletto of anxiety churned his stomach.

He went up to the marble shelf and rang the bronze bell to summon the head magician.

Without looking at him or even turning around, Cheops asked the magician if he had heard the latest rumors.

"Ah yes . . . Postpyramidal era . . . an ugly phrase, like so many you hear nowadays . . . I've spoken to the head of the security service about it . . ."

In Cheops's mind the silver platter glinted lugubriously before running with blood.

"I know," he said. "I also know what he thinks of the matter . . . But, even if it dismays us, there will be a post-pyramidal era one day, won't there?"

"Hm. I'm not sure what to say about that," the magician replied.

Cheops was tempted to remind him that he had opened his heart to him once before, twenty years previously, and the magician had told him that the pyramid was the pillar of the State, light condensed into stone, and so on. But he also recalled simultaneously that all those who had witnessed the scene were now rotting in the ground. How time passes! he thought.

"Well, what will happen when it . . . I mean, when the postpyramidal era comes?"

"Hm . . . Majesty, allow me to make one objection . . . There will be no postpyramidal era, for the simple reason that the pyramid will always still be there."

Cheops turned around abruptly.

"Djedi, don't evade the question," he said very quietly, though his words echoed in the magician's ears as painfully as a scream. "You know perfectly well that the current weariness and, so to speak, the dissolution of Egypt are due to the fact that the pyramid is nearing completion."

"A pyramid is never completed, Majesty," the magician replied.

"What's that?" This time Cheops really had screamed. "Am I going to have to build another one, as my father did? Or demolish half of this one so that it can be rebuilt?"

"No, Majesty! When I said that pyramids have no end, I was thinking of yours and none other. It has no need of a twin. Nor any need of rebuilding."

"All the same it is nearly finished."

He looked up to see if he could find the dust cloud on the horizon.

"Its body will be finished, but not its soul!" the magician continued.

He went on for a long while in such an even voice that Cheops very nearly dozed off.

"How many steps are there left to build before reaching the vertex?" he asked in a muffled whisper.

"Five, Majesty," the master-magician answered. "But the

Minister for the Pyramid was explaining to me yesterday that they get smaller as they go on. There are no more than two hundred and fifty stones left to lay, maybe even fewer."

"Two hundred-odd stones . . ." Cheops repeated. "But that means it's almost finished!"

The shout of joy that should have been uttered with these words turned into a shudder of fear. He tried to smile, but his lower lip would not budge.

"Two hundred and a few stones," he rearticulated in his mind. "How awful!"

Dust whirled up into the sky with ever greater force.

"A sandstorm is on the way," said Cheops.

Inside the palace the wind's whistling could not be heard quite so clearly. It was more like a rumble or a man's death-rattle. If someone had not thought to put away the papyri that Cheops had left on the balcony, they would surely have been blown far away.

Actually, he thought, the scrolls could go to hell.

Sand and rumblings, that's Egypt for you, his father Seneferu had told him the day before he died. If you master them, you master the country. The rest is just fiction.

It was especially when storms of this kind broke that these words came back to him. He listened absentmindedly to the roaring moan outside. It was as if Egypt in its wild-eyed, convulsed entirety, stirred up by the wind, was howling curses at him. He too wanted to yell: "To death with you! What demon has taken hold of you, O my mad kingdom?"

VII

Chronicle of Construction

Chronicle of Construction: fifth step, from the one hundred and ninety-seventh to the one hundred and ninetieth stone. From the report of Controller-General Isesi.

ONE HUNDRED and ninety-seventh stone, from the Aswan quarry. Nothing particular to report. Time taken to hoist to head of ramp: normal. Soldiers' graffiti: no political significance. (Two vulgar words referring to female genitalia, one of an affectionate, the other of a repulsive nature.) No veining or other specific marks. One hundred and ninety-sixth stone. From the Karnak quarry. Difficulties in raising. SALS (seal authorizing laying of stone) in order. Ordinary graffiti: penis. Nothing else to report. Stonelayer Sebu's impression of having heard a groan from inside the block was unfounded. One hundred and ninety-fifth stone. From El Bersheh quarry. Hoisting delayed owing to suicide of head stonelayer Hapidjefa. Tricked his workers into letting him use the stone to end his days. ("Leave this side to me, I'll take care of it while you have a break.") Following the west-face magician's instructions, the block was rotated so that the death-stained side faces outward. The sun's rays will bleach the evil out of it—presuming it has indeed been contaminated by Hapidjefa's soul. One hundred and ninety-fourth block. From El Bersheh quarry. Caused the death of four men in the desert. In very obscure circumstances. Despite this, hoisting was straightforward. Seal and other documentation in order. No problems in placing it, apart from last-minute loss of one of stonelayer Thep's hands. His own fault. One hundred and ninety-third stone. From the Karnak quarry. Seal in order. But setting delayed by graffiti reckoned by some to be insignificant but by others to be politically inspired. Transcribed as per rules and sent on down (that is to say, to a higher place). Copy taken for the Security. Another copy to CBPP (Central Bureau—Pharaoh's Palace). One hundred and ninety-second stone. From Aswan quarry. Despite having no special signs, proved difficult to hoist. Indirect cause of the crushing and subsequent death of carver Shehsh. (For reasons not known, he had spat on it as it passed step one hundred.) One hundred and ninety-first stone. From the quarry at Thebes. One face speckled black. Returned to quarry by special order. During its return to its place of extraction, it obstructed the ramp for half a day. But caused no deaths. The seal-bearer maintained that the speckling had appeared during hoisting.

One hundred and ninety-first stone, substituted for the preceding. From the quarry at Illahun. Nicknamed "Ruddy" during hoisting because of its reddish stains and veins. Nothing special to report. Time taken for raising: normal. Graffiti of no interest. One hundred and ninetieth stone. From Abusir quarry. Nothing particular to report.

Chronicle of Construction: third step, from the forty-seventh to the forty-fourth stone. From Security records. Marginal notes added by CBPP.

Forty-seventh stone. From Aswan quarry. Double check carried out as per latest instructions. Swearing heard during haulage: "You should burst like my heart!" "You should be smashed to smithereens!" "You should fall into the abyss!" Blessings heard: "Thank fate to have placed you on this peak!" "I wish you a long life of stone!" SALS in order. Magician's authorization ditto. No problem in hoisting. No graffiti. Forty-sixth stone. From Karnak quarry. A reliable seam. Cursing and praising in roughly equal measure. One of the latter kind of expressions—I sacrificed my son to the pyramid with joy—alludes to an accident that occurred during unloading of the stone. No graffiti. They have disappeared as a result of improved surveillance, a very successful measure. Forty-fifth stone. From Karnak quarry. Same curses as for the others ("You should tip off the top," "You should disappear into the void," etc.); praise similarly standard. Some confusion during raising because of Setka, the idiot that the foreman had permitted to sit astride the stone, shouting "Giddy-up, old nag!" The hullabaloo was thought to be of no consequence. Everything else normal. [Marginal note: the idiot's ranting may have been of no consequence, but some of his utterances had a double meaning. For instance, some of the urgings he uttered as he whipped the flank of the block: "Whoa, you filthy animal, get on with it!" "You're in luck, you are, to be going up so high!" "Where lie your father and mother? Down there, right at the bottom!" "Get a move on, slowpoke, what's holding you up, do you mean to say you don't want to get hoisted right up to the top? Did you think you were going to be the pyramidion? Poor old dimwit . . ." Subsequently, after the idiot had been made to come down, he blurted out these mysterious words: "This pyramid will grow a beard one day!" Despite a full day of the rack and a beating, he provided no further explanation.] Forty-fourth stone. From El Bersheh quarry. The only one of the four stones that fell into the Nile to have been recovered. Whence its nickname of Drownee. As for the rest, seals, second check, duration of hoist, laying—no problems.

Chronicle of Construction: penultimate step, from the ninth to the fifth stone. Extract from the records of the CBPP.

Ninth stone. Hewn at Abu Gurob, on the borders of Libya and Egypt. Seals in order but authority to lay held up by a denunciation. Suspicions that the stone had been switched during haulage. The stone was alleged to have been replaced by another taken not from the said quarry but from an old pyramid. Investigation demonstrated that the accusation was false. Eighth stone, from the same quarry. Of outstanding quality, like all stone cut at Abu Gurob. Which explains the jealousy that these stones arouse. First wind of denunciation at the quarry itself. Followed the stone to Medinet Mahdi. You might have thought that it would have faded away once the stone had been loaded onto the raft for the Nile crossing. But not a bit. It tracked it all along the riverbank and reattached itself to the stone when it was unloaded on shore. And it went on until investigation established that there was no foundation at all for the suspicion. Seventh stone. Also from Abu Gurob. Variously nicknamed Wild One, Blackstone, Bad'un. Also dozens of other nicknames after falling. Reasons for the slip not clarified. From the penultimate to the fifth step, it slid back down the ramp quite slowly, so it was first thought that it could be stopped. But once it reached the ninth step it began to accelerate. Crushed its first victims at the level of step eleven. Around step fourteen, it just went mad. Left the ramp, and, making an infernal racket, tumbled down along the pyramid face itself. The entire northern arris was badly shaken. At step nineteen panic broke out. At step one hundred and twenty-four, where the numbering reverses, it split in two. One half went off toward the right, the other carried on down. Ninety-two dead in all, not counting the injured. Other damage incalculable. Day of mourning for the pyramid. Sixth stone. From Saqqara quarry. Though it killed two men, it was an angel compared to its predecessor. Whence its nickname of Good Stone. Fifth stone. Also from Saqqara. Nothing in particular to report.

Appendix: re stone seven. From the Pharaoh's Special Envoy marked "Top Secret" in red.

Discovering the true causes of the fall of the seventh stone is of the utmost importance for the State. In the account of the actual facts there are contradictions that arouse suspicion. The team undertaking the investigation is paying particular attention to the following points: causes of the slip (were real attempts made to stop it while it was still possible to do so, or did people turn a blind eye?); precise description of the trajectory; reactions of men on site; acts of heroism and/or cries of fear ("The pyramid is collapsing!"); other suspect reflections ("The higher you go, the harder you fall," etc.).

Report of the Commission of Inquiry.

There is no lead on this seventh stone, neither from the quarry, nor through the usual channels of denunciation, including those used, mostly anonymously, by land-based and waterborne hauler. The start of the slip was almost imperceptible, to the extent that the builders leaning on it did not even feel it beginning to move. Head stonelayer Sham was the first to remark: "But what's going on, this stone feels as though it's shifting!" The others thought he was joking, and teased him back: "Hey, you must have pushed it"—"No, it was you," etc. A moment later when they realized that the stone was indeed on the move they tried to stop it with their bare hands, but to no avail. Then head stonelayer Sham, realizing that he had no grappling iron to hand, hurried to get one to slip it under the block. The others set to as well, but too late. The stone sent all the hooks flying and, as if increasingly angry, rushed headlong. It began to zigzag on the ramp at the level of step ten and began its massacre at step eleven. At step thirteen foreman Thut put himself in its path and yelled: "Long live the Pharaoh!" But he was crushed to pulp. One of his hands was torn off and went flying through the air, which only exacerbated the panic. When it reached step fourteen the stone left the ramp and went into free fall. It was at that point that stonelayer Debehen began to howl: "The pyramid is collapsing!" For reasons unknown he then hurled himself at the foreman and bit his throat. Others began rushing about in all directions as during an earthquake, but they were in such a state of terror that some of them, far from evading the stone, found themselves in its path and got crushed. By step twenty the bloodstains on the masonry block could be seen from far away; lumps of flesh and hair rained down with it as it fell. In fact it was not at step one hundred and twenty but slightly before that it split in two, and the witnesses who adamantly insist that it split at the precise point where what is called celestial numbering begins are either the victims of pure chance or the tools of some dark political design. The investigation continues.

VIII

Nearing the Summit

A S THE hot season set in, the view of the pyramid rapidly altered. The ramps were taken down one by one, laying bare the dizzyingly steep sides of the monument itself. Only one hoisting track was left in place, the one that would be used for the last four stones and for the king-piece itself, the pyramidion.

In due course the area surrounding the base was cleared. The barracks that had served as the stonelayers' sleeping quarters were dismantled, as were the redundant storerooms, messes, and stalls. Broken stones were gathered up and carted away every day together with reed-ropes, planks, broken winches, grappling tools, and all sorts of now useless rubbish.

The dust cloud over the building site began to lighten. But the sense of relief that resulted was not caused by the color of the sky alone. A new brightness spread in stages to the surrounding area, reached the capital, and even pushed on farther, to those remote provinces that good news, unlike bad, never reaches very fast.

Meanwhile the first taverns reopened, if rather hesitantly. Here and there, houses began to sport their numbers again. (It was rumored at the start that they had been removed to stop people finding their friends' dwellings, and so to prevent the holding of dinner parties.) It became increasingly normal to see charcoal graffiti saying, "We've built the pyramid! Now let's have some fun!"

Passersby nodded their heads. About time too, they said.

The flame of joy flickered but would not crackle, as if the logs in the hearth were still too green.

A single stone that had come adrift and tumbled down from the penultimate step had been enough to bring everything to a halt. Even without the investigation that the accident caused, those would have been very gloomy times. People felt that ancient, probably already dead afternoons had returned to cast their drab and guilt-laden light over them. Others imagined they were reliving a previous season. But even then they did not doubt that once the pyramid had been completed their field of vision would grow clearer and that things would find their right places again.

All the same the order to hoist up the last four pieces had still not come. Nor was there any mention of setting the pyramidion. It was allegedly being covered in gold leaf in some secret temple.

At dusk the ramp that would be used to push it up to the vertex looked like a fragile wire along which only spirits could travel.

Around the hut where the last four pieces had been stored

and which was now guarded by sentries, god knows why, people could barely hide their amusement. To be sure, these stones were more important than the others, since the pyramidion itself would stand directly on them, but all the same, they were only bits of stone, not ministers, to be guarded like that! Others thought quite the opposite, that ministers were only transitory things, whereas those blocks of stone would live on until the end of time.

The four last stones and the pyramidion were referred to as if they were living people. The quarry of origin of one of them was even kept secret. On its delivery, so the story went, it was still bloodstained from the body of a man it had crushed on the way. So what, some people said, even if it has killed a man! We all know that the journey from a quarry to the pyramid is not an afternoon stroll!

People with business in the capital came back full of news. New bars had opened, there was more and more writing on the walls. Today's youngsters, they said, young lads born at about the time construction started, were almost fearless. They had still been kids when the first step had been laid, so they had no knowledge of the first and most terrible stage of the work, before the pyramid had become visible.

Most people thought that that earliest phase was indeed the one that had been the most soul-destroying. Thereafter, as it came out of the depths, the pyramid had become less fearsome. It was even so obvious that when the youngsters reproached their parents for having been over-fearful, the older generation replied: "You are only saying that because you have no idea of what a pyramid is like before it can be seen." The young folk shook their heads in disbelief. They would have found the opposite more credible.

The notion that the pyramid had become less frightening as it had become more visible was perhaps the source of a wave of nostalgia for the first phase of the building work that spread among the stalwarts of the State, and particularly among old pyramid hands. Young people enjoyed poking fun at the veterans' hopes that the good old days would return. "So are you waiting for the pyramid to go invisible?" they would ask, with snorts of laughter.

The old hands smiled back. But not without irony.

The idea of building another pyramid at first seemed so crazy that it was attributed less to wistful veterans than to the ravings of Setka, the idiot who had been allowed to hang around the monument ever since the foreman had declared that there was no building site in the world that didn't have a cretin attached to it. But later on people recalled old facts that had seemed puzzling at the time and whose significance was now becoming clear. For instance, that the Pharaoh Zoser, after completing his own pyramid, had had four giant stairways added, thereby extending the construction work by seven years. Or that Seneferu had had three pyramids built, without ever revealing which of the three contained his tomb. From this it could easily be inferred that the imminent completion of one pyramid automatically gave rise to the idea that another one was about to be started from scratch. But a firm speech by the architect-in-chief referring in particular to the rumor about the possible birth of a new pyramid made it absolutely clear that the Pharaoh would entertain no such notion.

A fortnight later, the unbuilding of a part of the pyramid (there was talk in bars of reconstructing the topmost part, or even a whole slope, as a piece of cloth might be unpicked and resewn) was denounced with equal firmness, and it became quite clear that not a single stone of the pyramid would be touched.

All that the disappointed veterans could do now was to dream of the pyramid returning to the dust and muddle of its youth, but that seemed as unlikely as their own rejuvenation. At the same time, and to the great displeasure of the old-timers, the taverns where young folk gathered grew noisier; and, as if that was not enough, perfume sellers' stalls that had long been closed were allowed to reopen one by one.

One night a torch could be seen flickering for a long while on the northeastern slope of the pyramid. It swayed, grew brighter and dimmer by turns, like a ghost, but people watching it from afar would have been a good deal more scared had they known that it was the pyramid magician accompanied by a team of inquisitors who were wandering around up on high. They carried on until dawn, looking for something deeply hidden, to judge by the movement of the torchlight, something nightmarish buried inside at some unknown time, or even, and that would be far worse, some secret or crime that was tempted to come out into the light.

Some of the gossip doing the rounds of the offices and bars got out of Egypt with amazing speed. Spies still dizzy from learning long dispatches by heart rushed off to their lands and returned a couple of weeks later bearing new instructions. By the end of their homeward journeys they had sometimes forgotten part of the report they were supposed to deliver, or else, like soured beer that has been left for too long in the gourd, the report had changed shape of its own accord inside their minds, causing a good deal of puzzlement at headquarters.

The only one among them who had no such worries was the Sumerian ambassador. Neither the day's sweaty heat nor the cold of night, nor even soft-headed messengers, could alter one iota in the clay tablets on which his reports were consigned. If it had not been for the smoking chimney (it had created a new proverb in diplomatic circles: instead of saying, "There's no smoke without fire," foreign ministry officials now said, "There's no smoke without a dispatch"), everything would have been quite perfect.

All the same, after a week of high tension, the ambassador was now in a very good mood. He had just sent in his last report to the capital, perhaps the best report he had drafted in his whole career. Though it was past midnight and despite the pain in his hands from a couple of burns (the report had been requested with such urgency that he had had to have the tablets crated while they were still hot), he was at last lying beside his wife and, overcome with desire, began to caress her.

Later, when he had left his wife and lain down beside her, as he usually did after making love, his thoughts turned back to the report he had just dispatched. It crossed his mind that it would be cooling down as it went. Just like his wife. He imagined the desert chill seeping through the crates and into the tablets. And so on, until morning, when the report would be stone cold.

Who knows why, but, instead of overwhelming him after such labors, sleep evaded the ambassador. It must have been the report that was preventing his brain from finding rest.

He tried to clear it out of his head, but it occurred to him straightaway that if he tried to do the opposite, to recall every last detail of the text, he might well end up asleep.

It was not an easy thing to do. There were one hundred and twenty-nine tablets in all—a veritable monument, as his assistants had called it. He attempted to remember the first eleven, which contained a general sketch of the situation, but between the third and the seventh he had a vision that came from god knows where of a dead sheep and the dusty mirror in the hall of his uncle's house near Kyrkyr, not far from the capital, on the afternoon of his suicide.

The first piece of specific news was in fact set out in tablets fifteen to twenty-one, which informed the Sumerian government that all the evidence suggested that unusual events were to be expected in Egypt. He managed to repeat from memory virtually the entire gist of tablet eleven: the significance recently attached to an event as unremarkable as a falling stone, alleged to be the result of enemy action (in fact, observers are firmly of the view that the fall had been engineered by the Security Service itself) supports the idea that a new wave of State terror is about to be unleashed on Egypt.

The ambassador's analysis of the causes was a veritable masterpiece. It was expounded on tablets thirty-nine to seventy-two, which also constituted the heart of the report . . . Watch out, you fool! he shouted in his mind at the carter driving his heavy load through the night. Every time the ambassador dispatched a message he was tormented by the fear of the cart overturning. He would have been sorry above all if the heart of his report were destroyed . . . This point is on the line of the axis . . . that place was perhaps where . . . the funeral chamber! . . . O heaven, he groaned to himself, this

Egyptian pyramid will make us all ill ... However much you
may try to rid your mind of it, you can't help relating everything else to the pyramid ... His wife's vagina also seemed
somewhat frightening when he entered it, like a mysterious
place with perhaps, at the very end, a mortuary chamber.

He turned his thoughts back to the analysis of causes. He
had tried to explain as clearly as possible the notion that the
completion of the pyramid was apparently responsible for
a resurgence of life, which, in its turn, had led to a détente
or slackening of discipline that was of serious concern to the
Egyptian State. For a period ministers had given way to their
bad habit of blaming Sumer for everything and had tried to
ascribe this laxness to Babylonian influence. They had even
repeated the old analogy between the pharaonic pyramids
and the canals of Mesopotamia: though they seemed to have
little in common at first sight, or only insofar as stone has
some relationship to water, both served the same purpose,
that of supporting the structure of a State. These reminders
had led to an idea that was very damaging in Egyptian eyes,
namely that the canals of Babylon at least brought some
benefit to the people by irrigating the land, whereas the pyramids, being unproductive and thus entirely uncompromis-
ing, were the ultimate incarnation of unadorned power, etc.
So they had tried to account for the situation in those terms
and had eventually conceded that the decline came not from
Sumerian influence nor from Sumerian canals, but plainly
from the pyramid itself. Now that it was on the point of completion, it could not oppress Egypt as it had done up until
then. Egypt was seeking to step aside, to come out from
under the weight of stone—in a word, it wanted to escape
from the pyramid.

The third part of the report was its high point. Tablets ninety to one hundred and twenty-two. Possible solutions. Snippets from spies inside secret meetings. Rumors that a new pyramid was currently under consideration. About un-building and rebuilding one of its parts. About an investigation conducted into a fatal mistake . . .

The ambassador shifted onto his elbow so as not to fall asleep. How many times had he imagined as he dozed off that people were trying to take it down! Crowds of men and ghosts each taking hold of a stone and vanishing into the dark . . . The chief magician and the architect were there, imploring it to give birth. But it was barren. Like his own wife. Maybe they intended to build a twin? How much time would that take, step after step, O heaven!

It appeared that Egypt could not survive without this hump. That is how the one hundred and twenty-second tablet began. What was inscribed on it was the idea that if another pyramid were not built, or if the great pyramid were not repaired, then something else would be done. Yes, definitely, they would dismantle it . . . or else they would have another plan.

Tablets one hundred and twenty-three and one hundred and twenty-four followed on in his mind. Then tablet one hundred and twenty-five, hinting at false hope that made the rest seem all the more depressing. Number one hundred and twenty-seven was of that kind, and a little overbaked; the penultimate tablet was just as implacable, with a black stripe from the oven right across it, like a mourning armband. And the whole thing concluded with the main point, a veritable pyramidion, cut into the last tablet, that Egypt could be expected to have a winter of unprecedented terror.

The ambassador laid his head on the pillow, but it felt like a piece of earthenware that shattered on contact, destroying once again any chance of sleep. His mind went back to the wagon rushing across the Sinai desert. The clay tablets must have cooled down by now, and his whole report would be as cold as a corpse.

IX

The Winter of Universal Suspicion

A<small>LTHOUGH</small> no season was entirely free of mistrust, only that year's winter was and always would be known as "the winter of universal suspicion." The name became so firmly attached that at one point it almost seemed to be part of the season itself and to have taken the very place of the thing it described. In fact, that is nearly what occurred. Allegedly, when people looked up at the sky toward the end of the autumn, instead of observing, "Well, winter's here to stay," they would say, "Suspicious weather, isn't it?" or "Don't you think suspicion has come rather early this year?" Schoolteachers were even supposed to have had the children chanting out loud, "There are four seasons in the year, Spring, Summer, Autumn, Suspicion"; and so on. Thus, in spite of the preventive measures proposed by the scholar A. K., that is probably what would have happened. In his third letter of denunciation, A. K. stressed that it was his rival Jaqub Har who had first put about the idea of substituting the name for the thing, and that he possessed definite evidence, which he reserved the right to submit to the sovereign once it was complete, which showed that the degenerate linguist was about to make a pernicious proposal for redesignating not just winter, but time in general—in other words, that the word *time* should be replaced by the word *suspicion*. The third letter of denunciation went on to say that after the repeated failure of his efforts to make his wife pregnant, the incorrigible Jaqub Har had come to think that time itself was worn out in this world, and that since it was now living outside of time, humanity would soon be obliged to adopt a time from another world, presumably from hell, unless it was to purloin the time zone of dogs and jackals. That was therefore what would have happened despite all the preventive measures proposed by A. K. (of these, the eleventh recommendation was the emasculation of Jaqub Har), had investigations in hand not been pursued with redoubled intensity during the spring, with the result that, since the winter had been defined as the season of universal suspicion, the spring should have been called the season of hypersuspicion—and as for the summer, the climate became so much more oppressive that no epithet could be found to describe it, and that was even more the case in the following autumn, which was so much later than usual that people feared it would never come, a fear exacerbated, in the view of A. K., by the sinister theories of Jaqub Har.

That winter remained the only season to be designated in that way simply because, as usually happens, people tended to remember not the height of a curse but its two termini, that is to say its start and its end, but as in this case there was no sign of an end, what was mostly registered in collective memory was the brink of the abyss.

Normally, the greater the scope of an investigation, the greater need it had of deep foundations, just like a building. The gravity of an inquiry depended on the time and place of the crime. Though promptness could be impressive, investigating an offense that had been committed only two or three weeks before could easily make the facts seem merely ephemeral things. At the other extreme, inquiries into crimes committed forty years ago may well be superficially impressive as evidence of the great rigor of a State that lets nothing pass even if it has a half-century's silt laid over it, but, like an earthquake with a distant epicenter, they run the risk of diffusing anxiety and making it less intense.

That winter's investigation was of middling scope. It went back about seven years, on average, fully sufficient to terrify at least two generations.

What was most curious about it was its localization in space. Whereas the minutes of investigations normally referred to two kinds of space, the real kind (the tomb with the corpse, the scene of the murder, etc.), and the unreal kind, also called impossible space (the rantings of a demented mother-in-law, nightmares, and so on), the new inquiry was located neither in the one nor the other, but in both at the same time.

In brief, according to the official announcement the clue to the puzzle that the investigation was seeking to elucidate was to be found inside the pyramid, at a point located roughly between the one hundredth and the one hundred and third steps, to the right of the vertical axis, in the heart of the darkness where the stones were heaped upon each other in a boundless agony that neither human reason nor unreason could properly imagine.

The puzzle seemed both decipherable and indecipherable at the same time. It appeared inaccessible, since dismantling the pyramid was inconceivable—for most people, at any rate. It is true that some said: "What if, one fine morning, what with all the heat and the boredom, Cheops decided, just like that, to do the unthinkable, to do what no Pharaoh before him had ever dared? What if he gave the order for the pyramid to be taken down, step by step, until the evil was laid bare?"

The ambivalence of the puzzle terrified every living soul. It was only a few yards away, right there, under its stone cowl. It was in between the two forms of life, but not entirely in either one, like the unburied dead, or like a living person walking through the market arm in arm with his ghost, of whom you could hardly decide which one made the more terrifying sight.

What was now generally understood was the way it had all started seven years earlier, with the howling of a jackal on the night of a full moon. The animal had followed the block of stone from the quarry at Abusir, across the Saqqara desert, to the outskirts of Memphis, and the itinerary, as well as some other details, had now been corroborated by more than one witness. The magician Gezerkareseneb had spent a whole night wandering about the face of the pyramid with a flickering torch in order to make out the exact position of the stone, the place where its journey had finally come to an end. Comparisons between the data that he collected and statements by witnesses, and especially a study of the quarry's delivery notes, of the stone's bill of lading in the archives of the Ferries and Waterways Department, of the first and second control certificates, and the results of various complicated calculations that apparently had nothing to do with these documents, established the fact beyond any possibility of error that the fatal stone was the two hundred and four thousand and ninety-third piece in the south slope, or, in the recording system used in the general inventory, stone n° 92 308 130393 6.

The figure looked rather bizarre, but everyone paid much more attention to what might be hidden in the pyramid than to the block's actual number.

Most people imagined it was a papyrus, in other words a secret document containing some threat or blackmail attempt, or else a warning for the future in case time suddenly changed its direction or its speed, as Jaqub Har had supposedly foretold.

Despite the oddness of its number, the formal identification of the stone nonetheless damped down the general level of anxiety. At least people knew that they were dealing with a piece of stone that had been hewn from a quarry, cut and shaped by stonemasons, inspected by a benevolent or threatening inspector, certified by a seal placed on it by a warehouse official, loaded onto an eight-oared ferry, then hauled on a buffalo cart whose drivers, like all their fellow hauler, had bellowed, spat, and sworn the whole journey long, had got drunk or else had pushed some peasant girl into a muddy field by the wayside. (Sometimes, the attackers got themselves so covered in mud from head to toe that they could not tell who was who any more and ended up raping each other.) Then it had been past the officials who recorded goods arriving at and leaving from the central depot, more inspectors, dockers (who "docked" the stone by securing it onto the dolly that slid up and down the ramp), pullers and pushers, and superintendents, before finally reaching the stonelayers.

Scarcely more than four hundred men had had to do with it, six hundred at the outside. Since the stone had been hewn and placed seven years earlier, half of the unfortunate men who had taken a part in the laying of that stone were no longer of this world. So even if they arrested all the survivors, together with their families, acquaintances, and drinking companions, even going so far as to include their mistresses and those who had infected them with the clap, they would have bagged no more than two or three thousand people, a mere trifle in the human anthill of Egypt.

But such consoling reflections did not last very long. The original worries resurfaced, because of the number of the stone. To begin with it was noticed that the number contained two digits that were intended to exclude or perhaps to assimilate entirely the two pieces on either side of the accursed piece. But that was nothing compared to the misfortunes that followed: in all probability, the stone's official number was quite unrelated to reality. To put it another way, it was perfectly obvious which stone was involved, but for easily imaginable reasons (secrecy, disinformation to confuse the enemy, etc.) the number given was completely wrong. As was the row where it was believed to be situated. And also its coordinates of location with respect to the vertical axis and the plane.

That was enough to make it seem within a few days as if the whole of Egypt had been smitten with apoplexy. Fresh rumors emerged only tentatively, made their way with difficulty along the tendrils of the grapevine. There was talk of a different number. Some people said that, according to the latest leak, the stone had been buried much lower down, in step fifteen, somewhere near the level of the sovereign's funeral chamber. Then it was alleged that it was not just one stone that was involved, but a whole row, row number one hundred and four, or so it seemed. Then other blocks of stone were mentioned, then other rows or half-rows, all of which served to make everyone feel unsafe. Men who had been only too happy to reminisce complacently about the time when they had worked at the Abu Gurob quarry on stones for the tenth or the ninetieth row, or in the false door workshops, for there was nothing they could be reproached with ("Ha! in our time it was all good honest work, the suspicious stuff didn't start until later!") now ran away to hide as soon as they heard that the investigation was approaching their rows, or wrapped their heads in wet towels for fear of losing their minds.

Nobody was arrested meanwhile, but that was not a good sign either. The only thing that remained unchanged was that the streets and the markets were deserted. As always, the perfume shops were the first to be closed, followed in turn by the tanneries, the bars, and the inns.

"I see Egypt, but where have all the Egyptians gone?" was what the Sumerian foreign minister was supposed to have exclaimed, riding through the town in a horse-drawn carriage after a reception given by Cheops.

Since passersby gave him the slip, he ended up putting his question to Youyou the drunkard, the only person who would agree to converse with him.

"You want to know where the Egyptians have gone?" Youyou answered at last, his tear-filled eyes fixed longingly on the patio of the bar that had been closed. "Up my asshole, that's where. Where else do you want them to be?"

He made a charming sign to the minister's wife, then, after yelling at the coachman, made off with a wobbly gait.

Little by little, one by one, the investigation cast its net over them all, and they became a multitude greater than ever before. People who had never even worked on the pyramid, people who for health reasons had never set foot in a quarry or stepped onto a row, aged and twitching aristocrats who were now virtually incapacitated, society ladies who never rose before noon—all were now roped into the same fetid atmosphere and the same dust, all mixed in and muddled up with people who really had worked on the building site.

There was always one string of the investigation to tie someone up, to draw him out of his cocoon, and to take him four, seven, or fourteen years back to the time when his errors began. If it failed to tie its victim up straight away, then the victims themselves, in their attempts to escape, got themselves into a tangle, pulled the whole skein toward themselves, and were entrapped. So even as their bodies lay huddled in the warmth of their beds, their terrorized minds were up and out before dawn, just like the host of builders in bygone days, ready to start work under the torrid sun and the whip, in order to repent for their share of guilt.

Investigations proceeded into the false numbers. As a result, people wandered around the pyramid like blind men, each looking for his own stone or row, ceaselessly climbing up and down, muttering, "No, it's not this one, I fell at the forty-fourth row." They would hail each other with sobs, make accusations, and beg each other for pity in muffled tones. Some came up against the false doors and asked in voices that were now quite unrecognizable, "Is anyone there? So this is the kingdom of darkness . . . My god, how icy cold it is here!" And strange visions passed before their eyes.

It was now obvious that the almost-finished pyramid was the source of a dozen times more pain and suffering than it had been when it was an inferno of building work. When they looked upon it from afar in the mornings, and saw it so smooth and shiny, so cold and silent, with its perfect edges and slopes, people could not believe their eyes. How could the sublime form of the pyramid be a machine for crushing people all day and all night long? They came close to suspecting that once darkness fell the pyramid took itself to pieces, that the steps, the supporting masonry, and all the blood-stained and mud-encrusted stones moved out of position, that they threw themselves around in anger and tumult, in an indescribable chaos, to spread mourning and misery all around.

Meanwhile, the investigation proceeded. The numbers were still just as wrong as before, so that crowds continued to clamber up the pyramid. All around you could hear groaning pleas such as "O seventh row, may you collapse of your own accord!" or "O third row, O third, it was on thee that I was reduced to dust and knew my end!" alternating with noises of people shouting in their sleep: "Make way for number ten thousand two hundred and ninety-five! Mind your backs! Stone number ten thousand two hundred and ninety-five!"

The pandemonium was at its greatest at the point where the step numbering reversed. Hundreds of people wandered around at that level having quite lost their bearings and their sense of balance: those who looked up suddenly felt as though they were doing a handstand, and so did those who cast their eyes down. They clung to each other in desperation, tore each other apart, foaming at the mouth, and ended up bursting into sobs together.

The ambient chaos and the eddies of dust were so overwhelming that they all dreamed of nothing but order and respect for the rules, at any price. For instance, they thought of stitching onto the sleeves of their tunics, or even onto their backs, the numbers of the rows, or the stones, or the names of the quarries where they or their relatives had labored, so that no one could mistake them, and even the bean vendor would be able to see from his counter and yell: "Hey you there, from step five (or from stone five hundred thousand, or from Gurnet Murai quarry), don't cut in line!" The vendor or the policeman would be welcome to keep them in order as long as that served to end the haunting suspicion that hovered over every single person, and did so all the more when it came from the local cop who had been looking at you askance all week and, one stifling afternoon, when it became known that all who had worked on step seventy-seven were traitors, looked straight through you as if to ask, So you wouldn't be one of those dodgers, would you now? With numbered tunics, you could show him your sleeve (or if it were empty, wipe his nose with it) and say: I'm from step forty-one, got that? Find someone else to scare with your cat's eyes! You can't get anything on me, because you were still dribbling your mother's milk when I left my arm under the three hundred thousand two hundred and fifty-ninth stone!

As they chatted, it seemed as if something kept on forming and then dissolving in their souls, and as it did so, it seemed to change their feelings about the pyramid. One day they bowed down before its perfection and wished only to be integral parts of its system; the next day, they would curse the monument, holding it responsible for all their ills; then they would take full responsibility for their suffering onto themselves; then they laid it at the door of fate; and finally swooned with admiration once again, before going pale with hatred the next day, and so on, repeatedly.

Old legends, some engraved on obelisks but most of them handed down by word of mouth, which said that the pyramid symbolized the balance between heaven and earth, that it drew in the light of the one and the darkness of the other, that it was like a cavern where the two worlds sealed their pact, or their coupling, which was maybe even an incestuous one, or the devil knows what, were now interpreted differently.

There was not a shadow of doubt that something underhand was going on in there. Just as under the crushing weight of the masonry, light turned first into darkness and then into a prismatic sparkle, so adoration, after being carbonized into hatred, turned itself into something quite different.

However dulled their minds may have been, people grasped perfectly well that the pyramid was less well adapted to drawing down celestial light or semen than it was to consuming the whole of Egypt. It had already digested Egypt once before, some people pointed out, during its construction; now it was chewing the cud, like a buffalo munching his hay for the second time.

103

Some thought that Egypt's ingestion by the pyramid was a calamity, others saw it as a blessing. Out of the accumulation of sufferings and their compression, the latter claimed, a new Egypt was being born, a purer land, crystalline and sparkling. Happy are they who will be able to benefit from it, as we do!

Meanwhile the investigation proceeded, and, in keeping with ancient custom, blind horses were used to take the scrolls and the chests in which statements were filed to the temple of Amun, whence they were dispatched before sundown to the investigators' offices. There was supposed to be a vast muddle of the most disparate objects lying there: still undeciphered reports from the Trojan messengers, decayed teeth, the iron needles that the old woman Bent Anat used to abort prostitutes, stones from the very bottom step, all the names of the builders of the twelfth step (three thousand eight hundred of them), the piece of rope that the Sumerian ambassador used to hang himself long ago, crushed scorpions, palm leaves, poems with double meanings, sand from the oasis of Farafra, which was where the magician Sa Aset was suspected of having cursed Egypt the night before he left, and even the bones of that infamous jackal, the one that had howled after the stone—the stone whose name and origin were still equally and entirely unknown—on that unforgettable mid-October night when all this horror had begun.

Nobody, not even the investigators themselves, quite understood the criteria used for selecting and sorting the evidence. For instance, it was impossible to know why the crate containing the wheel recovered from the swamp at Behedet (the wheel was suspected of having belonged to the carriage of the Babylonian ambassador, the one who had delivered the vials of poison to the treacherous vizier Horemuya) also contained the poem *The Old Quarry*, by Nebounenef, together with the malicious interpretation of it written by his fellow-poet Amenherounemef, who claimed that the author's exaggerated liking for the old quarry of Luxor (where the stone of the first four steps had been hewn) was but an expression of his discontent, not to say of his resentment against the State, sentiments expressed transparently in the following lines:

> *Now all alone beneath the light of the moon*
> *You recall once again the days of your youth*
> *When you gave birth to pyramids . . .*

But even if that was pretty unintelligible, it was even harder to understand why they had put in the same file as the poem the Sumerian ambassador's wife's underwear, as well as the papyrus used to record the results of the investigation of the poor fool Setka, in particular his allegedly ambiguous claims about the hair that was supposed to grow on the pyramid one day, together with the investigating magistrate's questions: "So, now we have pulled all your hairs out, will you still not confess?" and the mental defective's replies: "I've nothing to add, I've said all I had to say, and as for that thing, it'll grow not just a beard, but eyes and teeth too!" Upon which his eyes and teeth were pulled out, which might not have occurred had the idiot not suggested it himself.

X

Topping Out

The Pyramid Demands Its Mummy

WHEN news broke that the pyramid was finished, the inhabitants of the capital, who were the first to hear it, were dumbfounded. A fair number cupped their hands to their ears.

"You said the investigation was finished?"

"No, not the investigation, the pyramid!"

"Oh, that pyramid . . ."

The dirt of a quite different kind of construction was still on their backs; their ears were still full of the echoes of relentless interrogations: You maintain that you never were on row eighty-one? that you said nothing to the hauler of stone number fifteen hundred and two? But why don't you confess? We know it all anyway! As a result, for a long while few people had cared very much about what was going on on the ground at Gîza.

Yet work on the pyramid had proceeded as in a dream, without a hitch. Dressed stone slabs were placed on the upper part of the north slope, and the other slopes that had inexplicably been left bare until then were also finished with limestone panels, progressively concealing the raw masonry blocks that had been hauled there from distant places under clouds of dust and secrecy; then workers set the four very last blocks that had been delayed for so long (the order was brought one afternoon by a black-veiled messenger); and finally, they raised the pyramidion to the vertex of the monument. It was the kingstone, dressed in gold leaf that sparkled even before moonrise, and it aroused an uncanny kind of commiseration. From the moment it was put into place until the dawn of the following day, people expected the sky to redden and bleed from being scratched by the pyramidion's tip: blood-rain should have trickled down the steps: but nothing of the sort came to pass. Without delay, as if they were cutting a newborn child's umbilical cord, workers dismantled the hoisting ramp that had served to raise the final stones, and thus removed the last remaining link between the ground and the vertex.

Although public attention had mostly been fixed on what was happening on the outside and at the top, far more extensive work had been going on lower down inside the pyramid. The black granite doors were locked shut, as were the false doors that people might have suspected of being real, as well as other entryways that it would have been wiser to consider as giving onto dead-end galleries had they ever been reopened, and so on. The "dead men," as the inside workers were called, suffered from incessant migraines. They pretended that they did not know the secret of the false sliding doors, nor of the ones believed to be real but which it was preferable to consider false, unless it was the other way round—and as a result they were permanently confused, and had no real idea, in the end, of what was what. They could not decide whether it would be better for them to take some initiative, or on the contrary to leave things to their fate; they would pace up and down, grinning, sighing, and scowling, as if they were demented, pretending not to be pretending, and eventually, at their wits' end, they would break down.

When they emerged pasty-faced on the last day of their work, and saw the soldiers waiting for them outside with axes in their hands, they understood how pointless had been all their meanderings in the pyramid's inner labyrinths, all their cunning, all their deceptions and their feigned gullibility at the sight of false doors, or of real ones that led to dummy passages, and so on. They finally realized that their fate had been sealed twenty years earlier, on that November day when the architect-in-chief, Hemiunu, had sketched the first draft of the pyramid's plan on a piece of papyrus. Height, orientation, gradient, axis, the distribution of the enormous weight of the masonry, and so on, had all been jotted down, and among all the many numbers and formulas there must also have been an unremarkable little sign, something like the letter D, for instance, D for "Dead," meaning them. Without their deaths, the self-enclosed, secure, and eternally impenetrable system that had been planned would not have been quite perfect. Which implied that their deaths had been inscribed from the start in the sacred formulas of the pyramid.

Perhaps each hoped even as he knelt before the soldier's

axe, perhaps he hoped until the very last moment that he would benefit from a stay of execution so as to join that small handful of men who would open the secret passage on the day the Pharaoh's body would be laid to rest in the pyramid. The architect-in-chief selected the reprieved with a wave of his hand. They were made to stand to one side: eleven men in all. All hope now lost, the others bowed their heads. Some left messages for their loved ones; most of them shouted "Long live the Pharaoh!" Only two yelled out "Death be upon thee, Cheops!"

People had expected blood to flow from the vertex because of the pyramidion scratching the sky, but instead it welled up at the foot of the mountain of stones.

At dawn the reprieved were taken in covered wagons to an unknown destination. As they drew away from the pyramid, their eyes remained fixed on a point near the summit where the exit shaft was located, the spot where, on the day of Cheops's funeral, after locking each of the doors from the inside, they would emerge into the light. They knew that they would meet death the very moment their heads came out of the shaft, but the summit was so high that the crowds amassed for the funeral ceremony would not be able to make out a thing, and certainly not the blood that would stain the top of one of the pyramid's four faces.

Anyway, that day was still far off. The idea that until then their lives would be tied to the Pharaoh's as by a chain of gold made them feel so joyful that they began to sing. Or rather, they thought they were singing. In reality, the sound that came from their lips was a terrifying croak.

▲

No official ceremony was organized, but most of the inhabitants of the capital as well as foreign legations came to look at the finished pyramid. While the foreigners oohed and aahed ("How majestic it is! How tall!"), locals shrugged their shoulders, exchanged nods and winks, restrained themselves from saying quite the opposite. In truth, compared to the other pyramid, the one they were in, whose stones and suffocating heat made them wilt and whose endless passageways they would have to wander for god knew how long yet, the one that rose up before their eyes looked stunted and far too smooth a thing, like a kind of wax doll—the kind that hints at the invisible and mysterious powers of demons.

They no longer knew which one was the real pyramid and which one was only its ghost. They would have been just as unable to say which one had engendered its likeness, and even less which one was in control of the other.

Nonetheless most people believed that the main pyramid was the other one, their own one, the one that was as murky as a column of smoke of unknown height and girth. But now and again, as they looked at its waxwork image, the blood froze in their veins and they almost burst into tears. Apparently each was as evil as the other. They must have been born that way, like twins, even if one of them was visible and the other was not.

Those who had had an opportunity to glimpse the model were even more horror-struck. As if to torture them, the pyramid now appeared all of a sudden in every possible shape. Until then, they had seen it continually changing its shape, like a nightmare vision. It had been born like a whirl of smoke, like a hallucination. Then it had condensed into the form of a model. Whereupon it had once more dilated, before changing into a black cloud and a conspiracy. And now here it was again, cooled and contracted, in the shape of a model. The devil only knew what shape it would take on next. Would it perhaps begin to jump back and forth in time, as in a witch's mirror, where real things cannot be told from their reflections?

Festivities had been expected for the evening of the inauguration, then on the following day, and thereafter until the end of the week. However, in place of invitations to the celebration dinner, the families of the reprieved received their relatives' excised tongues.

The capital shuddered. What horrified people was not so much the excision of tongues—a quite frequent practice, and a requirement for various high-ranking posts, notably in the police archives and in the palace service—as the delivery of the excised tongues by messenger, and, even more, the fact that the organs came wrapped in a papyrus bearing the pharaonic emblem.

Nobody failed to appreciate that what had been sent out was another warning.

As you might expect, Memphis was plunged into even denser silence.

The habit of keeping quiet reached such proportions that, according to a further report from A. K., Jaqub Har, the linguist, forecast that if the present trend continued, then half of the Egyptian language would have disappeared within three years, and within a decade there would be barely three hundred words extant, which could be learned even by dogs.

In fact the general buttoning up of lips was not based solely on fear. For a long while now things had become much more discreet, and even the bureaus whose job it was to spread rumors and induce panic seemed to have become tongue-tied. The royal herald's drum, even the creaking of a door or the clank of chains, now seemed not to make the sound expected of them. People complained of illnesses going back greater or lesser lengths of time. Some tossed in their sleep, unable to bear the thought that the pyramid's funeral chamber was still empty. Others groaned as they thought of the eternal imprisonment that the stones were suffering. They bewailed the stones' agony uninterruptedly, as if the tails of their tunics had been caught under one of them and were stopping them from ever moving away.

The sickness even affected what seemed to be the best protected from it—the investigations themselves! Sand began to cover the files; some prosecution witnesses were aging so fast that they had become unrecognizable by the time of their second confrontation with their victims.

Unlike the situation in the first few months after the pyramid's completion, the number of individual visitors was now increasing. In silence, each would seek out the row where he had been denounced, or conversely the row where he had denounced someone else. People would wander up and down, muttering, "No, it's not here, it must be farther on"; then, unable to locate the scene of the deed, they would be tempted to go back to the police station, to hammer on the iron doors with their bare hands, screaming: "Open up, open up, issue a summons, interrogate us, or we'll go mad!" But the offices of inquisition were also growing ever quieter. The interrogators now only hobbled about; they felt worn out; their eyesight had grown significantly weaker.

The sharpest minds tried to clarify the causes of this all-pervading decline. The exhaustion and the misleading glow in which everything was now suffused was obviously not easy to explain. Everything was unwinding and drawing back as if before a ghost. But the hardest task was to track down the lever or cog responsible for the sluggishness of a machine that was supposed to know no rest, that is to say the intelligence service. And it was even harder to pierce the reasons for this dense and alien silence that had enveloped both camps, persecutors and persecuted alike.

Some nodded skeptically. Don't go looking for explanations when there aren't any, they objected. It's the silence of the tomb, and nothing more. Every grave has its silence underground. The pyramid has its silence right up there.

XI

Sadness

PEOPLE spoke that way because they did not know what was going on in the Pharaoh's mind. Cheops was despondent. In the past, and on more than one occasion, he had had his black moods. Sometimes it only takes a single misfortune, such as the wrong turning taken by his daughter, to bring a man to his knees, but the Pharaoh's present torment was of a different kind. It was not just a bout of dejection, but a sadness as vast as the Sahara—and every single grain of its sand made him groan.

For a long time he pretended not to have any idea of what had thrown him into this state, and even denied its existence. Then one fine day he stopped hiding it from himself. His atrocious unhappiness was caused by the pyramid.

Now the thing was finished, it attracted him. He felt that he had no option but to be drawn toward it. At night, especially, he would wake up in a sweat, shouting repeatedly:

"To depart, O, to depart!" But where would he go? The pyramid was so tall that it could be seen from everywhere. From the distance it seemed to be on the point of calling out and saying: "Hey, Cheops! Where do you think you're going? Come back!"

He had had people punished on charges of delaying the building work. Then he had had others sentenced for the opposite reason, because they had speeded the work up. Then again for the first reason. And thereafter for no reason at all.

The day when they finally came to announce that it had been completed, he was completely dumbfounded for a moment, and the messengers did not know what to think. They had expected a gracious word, if not an expression of enthusiasm, or at the very least some conventional formula of congratulation. But Cheops did not move his lips. His eyes seemed to go quite blank, then his silence infected the messengers too, and they all stood there together as if they had been plunged into desolation, into the void.

No one dared ask him if he would go and see it. Little by little the palace went into mourning, as if there had been a bereavement. For several days no one ventured to speak of the pyramid in front of Cheops again.

The Pharaoh had contradictory feelings about the pyramid: he could feel its attraction while at the same time hating the thing. Because of the pyramid he had begun to detest his own palace. But he was not keen on moving into the pyramid either. He considered himself too young to go over to the other side, but not young enough to go on be-longing to this one.

On some days, however, he had a muddled and insidious

feeling that it was calling him. He changed his sleeping quarters several times, but wherever he went he could not escape its rays.

During the full moon he shut himself up for nights on end with the magician Djedi. In muffled tones, as if he was trying to lull him to sleep, Djedi told him all about a man's double, his *kâ*. And about his *bâ*, another kind of double that appears to a dead person in the shape of a bird. Then, in an even more trailing voice, he spoke of shadows and of names. A man's shadow was the first thing to leave its master, and his name was the last: in fact, the latter was the most faithful of all his possessions.

Cheops tried not to miss a word of what the magician was saying, but his attention wandered. At one point he muttered: "With my own hands I have prepared my own annihilation." But the magician did not seem at all impressed by this statement. "That's what we all do, my son," he remarked. "We think we spend our time living, whereas in fact we are dying. And indeed, the more intensely we live, the faster we die. If you have built the hugest tomb in the world, it's because your life promises to be the longest ever known on earth. No other place of burial would have been big enough for you."

"I am in distress," Cheops said. The magician's breathing grew heavy, as if before a storm. Djedi began to confess his own torments to the Pharaoh. "I am unable ever to forget anything," he said. "I even remember things that it is forbidden to recall. I can still see the darkness inside my mother's womb. And the claws I had when I was a wild beast. Instead of growing outward, as it does on all animals, my fur grew inward, into my flesh. I hear the call of the caves. I

117

am alone in knowing what I suffer, my son, I confide in no one. Your pain belongs to a different universe. Your torment is henceforth the torment of a star. You don't know what earthbound torment is. May you never know it!"

"I do not wish to know any other torment, even the torment of a star," Cheops interrupted. "Anyway I've begun to get cross with the stars."

"Well, that's hardly surprising," the magician replied. "That's something you are free to do. You are of the same race as they are. You'll have quarrels and then make it up. You're among your own kind."

Cheops cracked the joints of his fingers out of irritation. He began to speak again, but what he had to say was not very clear. He went on beating around the bush until in the end, all of a sudden, he asked the fearful question: "Couldn't we cheat the pyramid by putting in a different mummy?"

The magician's eyes opened wide with fright. But the Pharaoh still had enough of his wits about him to justify his question. He had been thinking of the possibility that his enemies might one day exchange his mummy for another, he explained. But he kept his cloudy gaze all the while on the magician's neck, and Djedi felt as if the Pharaoh was going to seize him by the throat, strangle him, and then wrap him in strips of linen cloth according to the embalming ritual.

The Pharaoh went on for a while about the risk of an exchange of mummies in the future. As if in a feverish dream, one question kept on recurring: Could the pyramid never be deceived? But the more he tried to justify the question, the more the magician became convinced that the sovereign was planning to put someone else to death and to put his mummy to rest in the pyramid, in place of his own.

118

The magician stared hard and long at Cheops, hoping to dispel his own anxiety. Then, in a deep, whispering voice he said: "The pyramid is not in a hurry, Majesty. It can wait."

The Pharaoh began to shake. Icy beads of sweat trickled down his forehead. "No," he groaned. "No, my magician, it cannot wait!"

The Pharaoh's mental derangement was kept secret to the end. Some days he remained completely prostrated and said nothing to anyone at all; but on other days, and particularly on other nights, he lost his mind completely. It was on one of those nights that he gave Djedi the magician a most terrible fright. Cheops declared that he proposed to go to the pyramid. On his own, and alive. So as to ask it what was making it howl like that in the dark, what was making it so impatient.

The magus had a lot of trouble persuading him not to go. All the same, with an escort of no more than a handful of guards, they did actually go one night to look at the pyramid on site.

It was quite still. Moonlight poured down from its vertex onto its sloping sides and illuminated the whole desert.

Cheops gazed at it in silence. He appeared quite serene. Just once he mumbled to the magician: "I think it wants me."

During the following days Cheops fell into an even deeper state of exhaustion. He babbled to himself for hours on end. At times he would wring his hands like a man trying to justify himself, seeking to explain why he can do absolutely nothing, no really, nothing at all, while his impassive interlocutor doesn't believe a single word.

▲

He died exactly three years after completion of the building work.

Sixty days later, after the funeral rites had been performed, his embalmed body was encased in a sarcophagus, and tens of thousands of people waited outside for hours on end, watching the great mountain of masonry.

Now that it had received the mummy that it was intended to house, the pyramid seemed to have achieved fulfillment. After consuming so many destinies, after devouring so many lives, it now rose up, haughty and triumphant, and sparkled in the sunlight.

A good part of the crowd that had gathered to gaze at it, and especially those whose sons or husbands had been convicted, recalled their loved ones' unending anxiety in the expectation of arrest, their last nights before being deported or sent to the quarries, the moments when they had been wrenched away from their families. They had subsequently learned fragments of what the deportees had suffered: interrogations, confessions under torture, dementia. Yet, curiously, that had not given rise to hatred among these people. They felt in a muddled way that as long as the pyramid was there, blocking the horizon of their lives, then neither hate nor love would ever manage to form in their breasts. An unhealthy evenness of temper and a wretched listlessness had taken the place of all other feelings, just as tasteless beans had long since replaced the more succulent dishes of bygone days.

All that they had lost only came to mind in vague and hesitant ways. Gay feasts among friends, love affairs, scandals, crazy poets chasing from one inn to another with their delirious words. All those things had progressively been eradicated from their own lives, blown away like so many shadows. The higher the pyramid had grown, the more distant all those things had become. They were so far away now, lost in nameless deserts and reed beds, that they could never find their way back.

One winter morning the new Pharaoh, Didoufri, announced the commencement of construction of his own pyramid to his ministers and closest advisers. Also present were Cheops's other son, Chephren, and his only daughter, Hentsen, who for many years had not set foot inside the palace from which she had been banned because of her misdemeanors.

All listened with tense expressions to the Pharaoh's words. The sovereign made no particular recommendation about the height of the vertex or the length of the arrises, and the assembled company was unable to decide whether that was a good thing or not.

Hentsen did not even try to hide her contempt for the behavior of the others. Latterly, people said, she had taken advantage of her father's senility to indulge in her latest whim—a pyramid of her own! It was rumored that she had required each of her lovers to supply a certain number of stones, so that people wondered just how many more lovers she would need in order to get her pyramid up.

There was a lot of gossip about this in the capital. People called it all sorts of things—the female pyramid, the shadow of Hentsen's cunt, its forward projection, the measure of its depth, a phallus demonstrating its receptive capacity, a vagi-nometer. She had wind of all these comments, but she was not bothered by them. She was even reputed to have de-clared: "Since the women of Egypt have gone frigid and given up sex, I shall make love for them all! May the pyramid prove that I am not boasting!"

The new Pharaoh was nearing the end of his speech. His younger brother Chephren, with his hairdo that was, to say the least, bizarre, was suffocating with jealousy and resent-ment. Oh, let my time come soon, he thought, consumed by bitterness. Let it at least come!

The thought of the day when he too could become Pha-raoh filled him with melancholy, as when one dreams of un-attainable things, and he was within a hair's breadth of bursting into tears.

Provided the day came for him to have his own pyramid, then people would see what stuff he was made of! He had discovered a very old statuette of a sphinx, which he hung on to like a fetish. When his friends asked him what was the meaning of his new hairstyle, where had he got the idea, and so on, he would just give an enigmatic smile. For it was the sphinx's coiffure.

He felt intuitively that this hairstyle possessed dark powers. He would do his hair that way for ever more, even when it began to thin out. Later on, for his own pyramid, he would have a giant sphinx carved in stone and placed at the base. A squatting lion with his own face. "Who art thou?" hordes of visitors would ask over the coming millennia. "Art thou Chephren? How didst thou become Pharaoh? What didst thou to Didoufri?"

But as we all know, the sphinx never answers questions.

XII

Profanation

A S THE ancient papyri tell, pyramids played their role as celestial go-betweens most particularly on nights when the moon was full. It was then that they would best capture the orb's wan and eerie glow and pass it on, drop by drop, to the depths of the earth, to the nameless black rocks encased in mud and void, and diamonds blinded by the light that they were unable to shed. The rays would also catch the skulls of the dead, lighting up their eye sockets for a second, before they went black again. Conversely, the tips of these monuments, with their granite pyramidions, spewed out god knows what ghastliness toward the sky— the kind of excrement of which the earth always has a surfeit and must relieve itself from time to time.

They now lay close beside each other over there, just as they had lived together previously in the forbidden city, during their earthly reign.

The pyramid of Cheops. At its base, the pyramid of his double, much smaller in size. The pyramid of Chephren, with its crouching sphinx. The female pyramid. Then, set some way off, the unfinished pyramid of Didoufri.

The female pyramid was the first to be broken into by robbers. It was on a hot and humid night. The crowbars trembled in the robbers' hands, for it was the first time they had ever tried to get into a monument of this kind. For several nights they had wondered which pyramid they were going to start on. Because it had not been possible to eradicate quite perfectly all trace of the secret entrances, they hesitated between the female pyramid and Didoufri's, which, as the tomb of a prematurely deceased sovereign, had been left unfinished; as for the former, it had been put up thanks to Hentsen's lovers, who, despite the fond memories they may have kept of their mistress, seemed not to have taken all the care required (probably because they had had a good part of their stones delivered straight after having slept with the Pharaoh's daughter, when the passion of even the most ardent lover is somewhat abated).

So they spent a long time trying to decide. There was not much to choose between them, with as many advantages and as many disadvantages on this side as on that. In the end they decided to profane the female pyramid, which, when all was said and done, looked the less daunting of the two. As they were accustomed to violating women anyway, an attack on the tomb of a woman seemed more natural to them.

They found it much easier than they had expected to locate the place in the wall where the main gallery began, and much easier also to remove the obstructions; as a result, by dawn they were very near to the chamber containing the sarcophagus. They were exhausted, and lay down on the ice-cold flagstones, waiting for dusk.

When at long last the night seemed to them to be thick enough, Bronzejaw (so named because he was the eldest) made the first attempt at operating the heaviest lever of the doorway's mechanism. But the black granite mass did not budge an inch.

"Go on, bitch!" he grunted as he gave another shove.

Unlocking the mechanism and the effort they then had to make to move the door panel drained them to such an extent that when they finally fell into the funeral chamber they barely had enough strength left to stay upright.

Bronzejaw was the first to stand up; then Toudhalia and One-eye followed suit. They knew from experience that torchlight always makes ornaments look more precious than they really are, so they held back from exulting prematurely. Bronzejaw ran his hand over the treasures in turn, saying only, between his teeth: "Whore! You whore!" After surveying all that was around him, he came back to study the sarcophagus. The others stood and watched as he slid his crowbar into a crack.

As they had predicted, the most valuable adornments were indeed inside the coffin. After they had gathered up all the precious objects and stowed them away in leather bags, the coffin and its mummy looked pretty dull and poor.

"Don't move the light about like that!" shouted Toudhalia to the torchbearer, for he could not bear to see the mummy's face. As a grave robber, he knew that once tombs have been opened, mummies sometimes ignite and burn to a cinder straight away, but he could not get used to it.

While he and Bronzejaw tapped the walls, hoping to find another door, leading perhaps to the chamber of offerings, One-eye leaned over the open coffin.

"What are you up to in there?" Bronzejaw enquired.

One-eye's one eye twinkled.

"I want to remove the swaddling to see her cunt," he said gruffly. "I've so often wondered what it was like, for people to make a whole legend out of it!"

"A whore's cunt, nothing more, nothing less," Bronzejaw grunted without turning round. "You'd do better to come and help us find the other door."

"What are you trying to do?" Toudhalia screamed in horror, believing that One-eye, still leaning over the mummy, was really going to remove the strips of linen.

"Her face is slowly turning black," One-eye observed. "I didn't think that happened to royal mummies."

"For heaven's sake, leave that mummy alone and get over here!" Toudhalia said.

He kept a close eye on his fellow-robber, fearing he was about to grapple with the corpse at any moment. But One-eye had got hold of a burned-out torch-end and was using it to scrawl obscene words and images on the walls.

"What a nutcase!" Bronzejaw exclaimed as he continued to probe the wall.

When they got to the opposite side of the room, covered with One-eye's graffiti, they found two lines of hieroglyphs over a crudely stylized representation of male genitalia, half-phallus and half-pyramid.

"What's he written?" Bronzejaw asked, for he could not read.

Toudhalia moved closer so as to decipher the script.

"Er . . . Ha-ha! One-eye is a funny devil!"

"Just read it to me, will you? You can giggle later!"

"Hee-hee," the other robber went on. "It's just smut. It says that the Pharaoh's daughter only liked pricks the size of a pyramid."

"He's a real nutcase," Bronzejaw remarked.

"It's an old quip," the torchbearer explained. "Do you remember Shabaka, who would dash off a rhyme for a drink? I think he made up that joke."

"You're both crazy!" Bronzejaw shouted. "Leave the graffiti and the quips alone, will you? Let's get on with the job, we've been moldering away in here for too long already."

Since they had turned around, they saw One-eye leaning on the coffin with one hand in the posture of a man about to vomit. He was as pale as a shroud.

"What's wrong?" Toudhalia asked.

One-eye looked as though he was about to faint.

"I'm not feeling very well."

"Then move away from there," Bronzejaw ordered. "You know the smell of mummies makes you want to throw up. It turns my guts too, you know."

"Let's get out of here, anyway. We can wait in the gallery."

"That's right. Come on, pick up the tools."

A moment later, they scuttled out. On the threshold, One-eye turned toward the sarcophagus one last time. "You old tart," he muttered sourly. "You only just got away with it."

For a long while their steps echoed in the gallery.

▲

Although they swore to themselves that they would never go into a pyramid again, less than two full seasons had passed before they realized that they could think of nothing else. They had acquired a taste for it, like tigers who, once they have had a morsel of human flesh, prefer it to all other meat. Ordinary tombs no longer satisfied them.

This time, apart from sharpening their crowbars and making all their other preparations, they also sewed several pieces of canvas into the shape of masks. They would soak them in vinegar and put them on their faces when the sarcophagus was opened. It was the only way to guard against the terrible sickness that came on when you got close to a mummy.

The profanation of the female pyramid (the strumpet pyramid, as they called it among themselves) had not yet been discovered, which gave them reason to act fast. But perhaps the robbery would never be noticed, since Hentsen's last lovers, those of her final years, had long since passed on and turned to dust. The sentries had also met the same fate; in fact, they had abandoned their task even during their lifetimes, since the money to support them had run out. But all the same the rape of the pyramid could come to light for some unforeseeable reason, and that would have made any further robbery very perilous indeed.

They had bolstered their confidence on the eve of the act with the thought that no one was interested in Didoufri's pyramid any more; otherwise it would not have been left unfinished. Their forefathers for several generations had earned their living as they did, as grave robbers, and had never got involved in politics, except by lending an ear now and again to barroom gossip. For instance, they sometimes picked up the information that this Pharaoh was more greatly honored than that one, though both had long been reduced to mere mummies and encased in their respective pyramids. Then soon after they would hear talk of the opposite. The one who had been more greatly honored was now relegated to oblivion, and people began to make wreaths and raise statues in honor of the one previously disregarded. These changes of tide flowed from matters political, so people said, but the robbers thought it all quite absurd and ridiculous—as if two mummies could get up from their graves, grab at each other's tunics, and scrap like tinkers!

They gathered in the pitch-black night at the foot of the pyramid and wasted no time in levering up a stone that, according to them, concealed the secret entrance. They had a lot of trouble this time, and they had to shift more than a score of stones. It was almost dawn before they finally found the passageway.

That was the hardest part of their job. Thereafter it all went the same as in the other pyramid. Before opening the coffin they covered their faces with the canvas masks they had made, with openings for their eyes. For a minute they larked around, scaring each other with these hoodlike contraptions.

While the others scooped up the funerary trinkets placed in niches in the walls, One-eye, as usual, lingered over the sarcophagus.

Bronzejaw was the first to look at him.

"So what are you up to with the mummy this time?"

"Come and have a look," said One-eye.

They came over and saw that One-eye had stripped the linen bandages off the mummy's face. Toudhalia and the torchbearer screwed up their faces in disgust.

"Just have look at these marks," One-eye whispered. "You can see right away that the man was strangled."

"Hm," muttered Bronzejaw as he leaned over to look more closely. "My word, you're right. He had his neck wrung like a chicken."

"What? What are you saying?" the torchbearer exclaimed.

"What are we saying?" Toudhalia repeated. "He had his neck wrung? A Pharaoh had his neck wrung?"

Bronzejaw's eyes clouded over.

"Listen here," he said. "We're just plain robbers, and this has nothing to do with us at all." (His voice trailed off into a tiny whisper.) "These are matters of high politics. None of our business, OK? And you!" he almost roared at One-eye. "It's not your job to examine mummies' necks! No one asked you to! Right?"

"Sure, sure," One-eye conceded. "That's enough bawling, you'll rock the pyramid."

"I'll bawl louder still if I want to, got that? You must know that stuff like that could get us the chop! What did Tut the Hobbler get done in for? Why were Beetroot and his brother strung up? All their lives they jimmied doors and nothing happened to them, then one day, just a hint of politics in some dive, and they were done for. No politics on my patch, you hear that? If it itches, go scratch yourselves somewhere else, but don't cross with me. Have I made myself plain?"

"All right, all right," One-eye said. "We've got you loud and clear."

It was still dark when they came to the exit. The stars were beginning to fade. They left their masks inside the gallery and came out in line. It was quite chilly. Toudhalia, who was expert in walking without leaving footprints, also destroyed the traces of his fellow-robbers' passage. He could not quite get over what he had just heard. A Pharaoh with his neck wrung . . . "The bastards," he muttered to One-eye between his teeth. "They must have squabbled worse than we do over those kinds of jewels."

Toward daybreak they were trekking alongside the pyramid of Chephren. The sphinx was still shrouded in darkness. Only its hair—the hair that had given rise to so much gossip—was visible in the first rays of daylight.

They quickened their step, for they could not have stood the stare of the sphinx. By the light of the moon, people said, it could drive you out of your mind.

One-eye brought up the rear. His head felt as though it was going to burst. He could not get the marks of strangling on the mummy's neck out of his mind. They were sure to come back to him in his dreams.

One last time he raised his eyes toward the sphinx. The morning sun had now reached its eyes. Their blank stare froze him as it had never done before. He wanted to shout out: "Sphinx, what didst thou do to thy brother? How didst thou kill him?" But his voice was stifled in his breast.

XIII

The Counterpyramid

THE FIRST attack on it came one December afternoon. A solitary shaft of lightning that had escaped for sure from the alien skies of the north fell upon it, but at the last minute, for reasons never properly understood, it split in two and, with an apocalyptic clap, shattered in the surrounding desert.

This first demonstration of its manifestly inviolable pact with the heavens aroused a profound sense of joy in the whole land. No one was aware that what the heavens could not do had been achieved already from below, by the men who had surreptitiously made their way into the pyramid.

The robbery had taken place years before, but since all trace of the profanation had been cunningly hidden, no one had had a clue. Maybe the truth would never have been known, had it not emerged where it was least expected—at a trial of writers.

When a group of scribes was arrested on suspicion that they were elaborating certain unorthodox historical conceptions, everyone expected a particular kind of trial, of the sort usually followed by high society or even by members of the diplomatic corps, in which the men in the dock are less the object of judgment than the ideas that they hold.

While an awkward moment for the educated classes was thought to be in the offing, news broke like a thunderbolt that the Historians' Affair was not at all a glamorous trial of intellectuals but a case that boiled down to nothing more than an abominable, unprecedented act of burglary . . .

People hearing the news for the first time went pale and weakened at the knees. Mummies had been stripped and profaned! Evil had scaled new heights. It had entered the realm of shadows. Everyone was gripped by a sense of sinister horror. Death itself had been robbed, so to speak.

It was so serious that many could not bring themselves to believe it was true. Had Egyptian historians sunk so low as to swap their styluses for crowbars? To go in for burglary in the middle of the desert?

But on the heels of this first confused and sensational version of the story came clearer and more precise details. The detectives on the case had found not only that the secret entrances had been dismantled but that the sarcophagi had been opened. The vinegar-soaked masks used by the bandits had been found at the site, as if they had wanted to be rid of them before running away.

The robbers had left the mummies where they were, thank God, but only by fortunate chance. For the mummies themselves must have been the target of the most shameless intention of all. The mere thought of it made people shiver. No one could say exactly what the robbers had planned to do with the mummies. Some thought they had meant to burn them, as barbarians do. Others reckoned that they would have taken the mummies to the far-off lands in the north, to put them on show, on kinds of platforms, and then auction them. In the highest circles, however, it was thought that this affair had more serious ramifications than appeared at first sight.

What aroused public curiosity above all was the way in which the group's machinations had been brought to light.

In actual fact, a veil of uncertainty periodically enshrouded the case. The accused, like most educated people, were hardly very vigorous; indeed, they were rather rather puny men, so it was not easy to imagine them handling great levers and shifting huge chunks of pyramidal masonry.

The secret police, concerned at people muttering such things, leaked sufficient details to clarify part of the mystery, specifically concerning how the discovery had been made.

It had all begun in a very ordinary way. For some time already the police had been in possession of a file on a group of scribes who were putting about new and rather bizarre ideas about the history of the State, not in accordance with official thinking. Although the authorities had alerted the palace, the affair had apparently not been considered important, so everything had stayed in the air. However, an anonymous letter—thank heavens, papyrus now allowed people to write letters, and, even more importantly, to deliver them with ease, for a Sumerian would have needed ten or fifteen clay tablets, not to mention other peoples who were still carving on stone and would have needed a pair of buffalo to haul their letter to its addressee, leaving aside all the other nuisances, such as the din of hammer and chisel that would have kept a whole neighborhood awake for a week!—an anonymous letter, then, had warned the Pharaoh, Mykerinos, of this new danger.

That was all that had been needed to get down to work. One spy and two undercover agents who infiltrated the group collected all the material that was needed, so that one fine morning, before daybreak, the ineluctable result occurred: arrests were made.

The inquiry was set up straight away, in utter secrecy. What the detectives were really after was to know where the young historians had first got their idea of questioning the official history of the realm. When after a variety of forms of torture the historians finally admitted that their crime had had its first beginning in a conversation with grave robbers, the upshot of which had led them to revise their conception of History from top to bottom, they were suspected of thumbing their noses at the authorities. They were put on the rack one more time, and were also the first to be subjected to a new truth-extraction device that had only just received its approval certificate. But although they found it difficult to articulate properly because of their swollen tongues (caused by scorpion stings), they mainly repeated what they had already declared: the idea of rewriting history had been suggested to them by an inebriated robber in a sordid bar called The Crab. They were tortured again, but were as pigheaded as ever, repeating their original version of the story (in writing, at this stage, since their speech had become incomprehensible—as bad as Sumerian!) and also gave away the name of the thief, a certain Abd el-Gourna, also known as One-eye.

The old reprobate was tracked to his lair, but, despite being half-drunk when clapped into irons, he had the wit to make it clear that in reality he had only ever seen the welts on the neck of the mummy of Didoufri in his dreams.

Nonetheless, toward dawn the next day, he finally confessed, and the investigating team took the man in chains back with them to the profaned pyramid. They moved aside the stone that hid the granite panel that blocked the entrance to the main gallery, they went inside, past the vinegar-soaked masks that still lay on the floor, to the funeral chamber where, with bulging eyes, they looked upon the open sarcophagus—when the head palace messenger rushed in after them with an order from the Pharaoh to desist forthwith from inspecting the mummy.

New veils of mystery enshrouded the case thenceforth. But as often happens when too much trouble is taken to keep something secret, the truth trickled out fairly soon, and more or less everything that had been in the historians' minds became common knowledge. Their plan had indeed been a gruesome one: they had intended laying their hands on all the mummies in the pyramids, transferring them to some discreet lair in Egypt or abroad, and submitting each of their organs to minute examination. From the evidence that they might thus uncover—throttle marks, knife wounds, traces of poison, etc.—they would throw new light on any number of events, whose explanations might then be linked to other prior or subsequent facts, which could reopen the whole established history of the kingdom. History would thus be rewritten into something radically different, and people said that in searching the prisoners' papers the detectives had come across phrases that might have been intended as book titles or as slogans, such as "History as Revised and Corrected by the Mummies," "Mummo-History," or simply "The New History."

There was a sickness floating in the air. The historians and the grave robber el-Gourna were long since dead and buried, but the disturbance they had caused lived on. Opinions never previously heard of were now uttered in places you would have least expected. At night, for no obvious reason, people with faces painted white wandered around the town. The number of seers and ranters increased dramatically. They could been seen haranguing onlookers in public places for hours on end. The only thing that could shut them up was the sight of the forces of law and order.

Everything was up for grabs, and the pyramids first of all. Now that they had been profaned, it seemed easier to express a view about them. People even began to question the correctness of their stellar orientation, of their locations, of the angles of their slopes. Even more fundamental queries were raised concerning the mysterious numbers and the coded message that they were supposed to contain. If this message was what it was supposed to be, why did it secrete a kind of vertigo?

"Come to your senses," replied other people—those others who in all times and circumstances take the side of the State, even when they are its victims. "Can one doubt the pyramid? It is the incarnation of Egypt. Without it, Egypt would not be what it is. Egypt might even not be called Egypt."

Nonsense, replied the doubters, Egypt existed before the pyramids. And has anything so awful befallen the Babylonians, the Greeks, or the Trojans, without their pyramids?

"Shush! Be quiet! You dare to liken the motherland to the handful of peasants that constitute Greece and Troy? If I were you I would ask for a pardon for words like that."

A time came when the confusion about the pyramids was so great that people began to wonder whether they really existed. They were alleged to be mere phantoms, collective hallucinations, mirages that would simply vanish into thin air one fine day. Some people went in for an even subtler analysis, saying that the pyramids, though they did indeed exist as such, reflected the wrong image of themselves, for there was always either something missing or something extraneous in what could be known of them.

However illogical these arguments may seem, more and more often (not just at dusk or in the half-light of dawn, but in broad daylight too) the pyramids appeared to be turning themselves into insubstantial objects made of air. That was now such a frequent impression that many people acquired the habit of looking toward the horizon each morning on waking, apparently uncertain whether the things would still be there.

The notion of immateriality notoriously suggests another, even more serious idea, that of pure and simple absence. Though it still hovered in a state of vagueness, as if it did not quite dare to come together, this latter idea did indeed begin to condense here and there. Could Egypt survive without its pyramids? Could the pyramids disappear? Could space be free of their ghastly protuberance?

People said "pyramids," but it was not hard to guess that they meant "Pharaohs," and they eventually gave free rein to their thoughts by alluding directly to a sovereign. Obviously not to the living sovereign, Mykerinos, but to a dead one.

To begin with, the target of their talk was not at all clear, but soon the buzzing converged, foreseeably enough, on the one whose pile of stone was higher than all the others, namely Cheops. The first graffiti were not particularly inspired (*Hump off Cheops!*), but it was soon realized that the forces of law and order were always too late by the time that they got to the defaced wall. When the clean-up teams came along with their buckets of whitewash, the crowds grew bolder and began to throw blunter insults at the pyramids. It became obvious that, for reasons that the State alone could clarify, a revision of the figure of Cheops was unavoidable. Many thought the required change had been dictated by foreign policy considerations, others believed that it was in order to redirect the surge of discontent onto a corpse, but very few ascribed it to plain and simple jealousy, aroused by the unusual dimensions of Cheops's pyramid.

In actual fact, far more outrage was expressed about the monument's size than about Cheops himself. Upper and Lower Egypt alike were in unprecedented turmoil and chaos. Previously placid and slow-witted folk—just ordinary bakers or clothiers—started to wake in a start, in high dudgeon, eyes bulging, bursting with indignation. "I was only a mere strip of a thing when they were building the pyramid, but I came close to using my bare hands to smash stone number two thousand eight hundred and three on the eightieth row!" Others told of their exploits, of how they had cursed row forty-nine, or pissed on row fifty-three, or indeed, of how on one dark night they had muttered "Go to hell!" and so on. In Memphis, in city-center bars, poets recalled the lines they had written and which, they claimed, contained anti-Cheoptic allusions—and the fear they had felt, for that reason. Amenherounemef, his eyes now watery with age, told of the terrible beating he had been given for composing the following couplet:

I saw the gulls leave on the wing
And could not restrain a tear

"When I think what I had to go through! I really thought I would go mad, what with my wife who kept going on at me: 'Retract, or you'll bring us all down. Can't you see how the others are keeping their heads down? Look at Nebounenef!' "

A person in the crowd of listeners remembered that it was actually Nebounenef who had been sentenced, on the basis of Amenherounemef's denunciation of his rival, and was about to open his mouth to remind the poet of this fact when his addled mind suddenly went blank and substituted a remark of a quite different kind, along the lines of "My back's killing me" or "I've been constipated for three whole days." A moment later he heard the word "gull" again, recalled what he had meant to say, but, being too lackadaisical to interrupt, began to yawn very noticeably while muttering under his breath: "Dog eats dog and I don't give a damn."

It was the same scene in every bar and every temple forecourt. Men who had yelled for all their worth, "We are innocent, we have always been loyal to the Pharaoh" before being sentenced to a stretch in the quarries, now shouted from the rooftops, "We were guilty, we wanted to undermine the pyramid, but they didn't let us!" Some people turned up from far-off provinces, from Aksha, Gebel Barkal, and even the fifth cataract, gave the names of the quarries or the number of the row where their loved ones had been sentenced to labor, as well as the names of the people who had denounced them. They brandished papyri under priests' noses, yelling: "We don't want national reconciliation, we want the files opened!" And they asked for reparations or for revenge, indeed for both at the same time.

Woe betide us, will we never escape from the pyramid! sighed the old hands. There they still were, perching on one or another of the slopes, beating their breasts, recalling imaginary exploits and tortures, until one of them, as drunk as a drowned newt, let rip with an old song:

> *When you sold me to row seven*
> *Your heart must have jingled with joy*
> *You old whore!*

The Pharaoh was kept aware of it all. Reports on public opinion grew increasingly gloomy. Informers got earache from such a quantity of eavesdropping, but that didn't change matters one bit.

One morning a man who had had an important dream was brought before the Pharaoh: a dream of Cheops's pyramid covered in snow.

No one dared to suggest an interpretation. Everyone was afraid of snow. Mykerinos himself put his head in his hands: he could not manage to work out whether it was a good or a bad omen. Many others recalled the lightning of long ago, which had perhaps been less an act of aggression than an appeal for understanding. But after that first misunderstanding, it seemed, the skies of the cold lands had sent snow.

It was obvious that the pyramid was in relationship with the outer world. If it had managed to attract snow from the fearsome northern regions, that meant that it had long been traveling back and forth between here and there, whether in thought, in dream, or by some means that no man could know.

XIV

Aging

A Pretense

A T CLOSE quarters, and especially if considered from
within, each storm-tossed generation possessed its own
distinctive features, but to the eye of an outside observer—
in the stony eyes of a statue, so to speak—the generations
of Egypt were no more different from each other than
desert dunes.

Dozens had come and gone beneath the unchanging lord-
ship of the pyramids. They were the essential things that
people found at their birth, and the main things that they left
behind them. The emotions that the pyramids aroused in
men were also cyclical. Admiration turned to indifference,
hatred, destructive fury, then reverted to indifference, followed by veneration, and so on, ad infinitum. The two broad
classes of feeling—favorable ones, and hostile ones—were
locked in a millennial duel, as it were, in which neither would
ever get the upper hand for good. And so it was with the

pyramid of Cheops. Although the rumblings of discontent that it provoked did not prevent other pyramids from being built, they did put a stop to any further growth in their size, and even prompted some reduction. As though they were trying to avoid being drawn onto dangerous ground, later Pharaohs declined to build pyramids as tall as Cheops's. That was the one that good and evil always stumbled over in the first place—as occurred, for instance, on that fourteenth of February, when a ragged fellow stopped in front of it after wandering about the desert for days on end.

For all the pages of transcription of the fellow's speeches that they made, the inquisitors never managed to establish who he really was. Was he just one of those nameless vagabonds who shift and vanish like waves of sand, or an unthroned Pharaoh, a eunuch, a mathematician, an epileptic, or a ragged astrologer on the run from an asylum?

He went on howling at the pyramid for a good while, hammered and head-butted the ground, screamed with laughter, pulled faces, and then smoothed out the sand with the flat of his hand and began to trace geometric figures in it with demented intensity. He sketched numbers beside the drawings and plunged into endless arithmetical calculations.

He obstinately rejected the accusation that he had wanted to damage the pyramid: his sole intention, he maintained, was to bury it. It was dead, don't you see? You could tell from a long way off that it was nothing more than a corpse. And like all corpses it had to be buried.

By his own account, he had spent hour after hour working out the dimensions of the trench that would have to be dug in order to bury the pyramid, the amounts of earth that would need to be shifted, the number of men needed for the excavation, the time the job would take, and so on. It would require more time than it had taken to build the thing, so that a new dictatorship could well take advantage of the dismantling of a pyramid, just as the old dictatorships had made use of its construction.

Not one single time did he answer precisely the questions that were put to him on the meaning of these last remarks. Nor did he ever explain what he meant by a dead pyramid.

"Stop laughing at us!" the inquisitors screamed, though the man was not really laughing at all, despite the twisted look that his torturers had put on his face. You could see straight off that it had stopped living, he kept on saying. "Just have a look at it from a distance. The idea that gave it life has gone, don't you see?"

He used the wall of his prison cell to carry on with his calculations, concentrating now on the natural wastage of the pyramid. The sums were even more complicated than before, because he had to allow for the gradual wind erosion that would affect each of the faces at different rates, for the variation between maximum and minimum temperatures, the levels of atmospheric humidity deriving from the close proximity of the Nile, right down to bird droppings and reptile friction, which, despite the relative infrequency of snakes, would nonetheless play a part in weakening the stone over about a million years—for that was the approximate length of time that it would probably take for the pyramid to crumble to nothing.

"Time!" he mumbled, as he slumped to the foot of his cell wall in sheer mental exhaustion. "Time alone will rub you off the face of the earth!"

▲

In truth the pyramid was aging, but at an infinitesimal pace. Its changes were not visible to the naked eye, apart from the rapid loss of its white sheen, which soon turned a dull pink. The first wrinkles appeared after eight hundred years. A stone on the west face was the first to split right through, one December afternoon. Six others, lower down in the supporting structure, had shattered before it.

It was probable that many others had gone the same way, but they were buried so far inside the edifice that no observation was feasible. Even when a dull thud was heard from the outside, it was never possible to ascertain the exact position of the implosion nor the specific masonry pieces that had been damaged.

Before the first visible signs of degradation occurred, fourteen stones on the northwestern arris turned a shade of gray. Erosion first became clearly perceptible some two hundred and seventy years later. It was not just the gray blocks that showed signs of weather-beating, but the whole array of which they were a part. It was the side most exposed to the desert wind, so that even though the stones used had been among the hardest available, from the Aswan quarry, the weathering was expected and surprised no one.

One hundred and twenty years later, mauvish-gray streaks appeared on a number of pieces on the south face, some of which also came out in pustule-like blisters. The pattern of streaking was completely irregular, which made it all the more difficult to work out its cause.

Signs of erosion began to be perceptible from a distance after one thousand and fifty years. Not just on the north face, ground down by the prevailing winds, but on the east and even the south face too, there were quite varied symptoms of decay, ranging from spongy patches to cracking, channels, holes, and, here and there, small slippages. That is how people came to talk a great deal about one stone on the north face where erosion had gouged out what looked like human features—a bulge that suggested a cheek, lines that could pass for eyebrows—as if some buried face was trying to get out from inside. Gossip about it even reached the palace, and appropriate measures were carefully considered: whether to intervene (with chisels, or more sophisticated instruments) to make the head emerge at greater speed, as was done at childbirth, or to wait patiently for the face to come out of its own accord.

Since the Pharaoh attached importance to the omen and was impatient to know its meaning, he favored intervening, but the High Priest was of the opposite persuasion: profaning the pyramid in such circumstances could have fatal consequences, he said. They agreed therefore to leave things to follow their natural course and posted sentries near to the stone to watch over it night and day. But as time passed the head began to lose its features, as if the unknown visage had had second thoughts and had decided to pull back into the inner depths. Many people were disappointed, not to say cross; others breathed a sigh of relief.

Notwithstanding these phenomena and their interpretations, people were scarcely conscious of the pyramid's aging. The first to give voice to such a notion were the members of a Greek mission. On first setting eyes on the monument, without even going close enough to see the details, they declared as one man: "Oh! but it's begun to grow old!"

149

It is hard to tell whether they said this with regret, with malice, or with satisfaction. The main point is that their words spread mayhem all about. People suddenly felt as if they could see clearly what they had failed to notice up to then: seen as a whole, the pyramid was no longer white and smooth as it was portrayed on old drawings; its four faces were all wrinkly, as if its skin had been damaged by eczema.

But that was only a fleeting impression. Long after, like a mature woman who proves her vitality by having a child late in life, the pyramid, despite being four thousand years old, began to reseed itself in distant places.

Flashes of light, hazy visions racing over the horizon, impossible ideas jostling each other before being carried far and wide on the wind . . .

That was when people recalled the dream of a pyramid covered in snow, the dream that had first foretold of the pyramid's shadow falling on the whole of the terrestrial orb.

XV

Skullstacks

LIKE A reflected image, the first avatar of the pyramid's afterlife occurred at a different time, in a place many thousands of miles away. In deepest Asia, in the steppe of Isfahan, a potentate called Timur the Lame raised a pyramid just as Cheops had done before him. Though Timur's was made of severed heads instead of stone, the two pyramids were as like as two peas in a pod.

Like its Egyptian predecessor, Timur's stack had been built according to a plan, with the same number of faces, and just as the stones for the first pyramid had had to be quarried in several different places, so Timur's seventy thousand heads, since they could not have been taken from a single war or just one *qatl i amm* (general massacre), had had to be gathered from the battlefields of Tous and Kara Tourgaj as well as from the slaughters of Aksaraj, Tabriz, and Tatch Kurgan. As in the old days, inspectors examined the heads one by one, since the skullstack was supposed to be made exclusively of the heads of men, though it is probably true that the greedy rummagers who delivered the skulls to the site sometimes tried to cheat by shaving the hair and muddying the faces of murdered women, so as to make them unrecognizable. The builders used mortar, but the architect, Kara Houleg, was not confident that it would suffice to protect the monument from the effects of winter weather and wild animals, so he had the skulls pierced and each row strung together, to prevent them being pulled apart by the wind or by wolves. That was how the first twelve rows were put together one by one, followed by a further twenty-two, and then another score, topped by the seven final rows. But they ran out of heads for constructing the vertex of the pyramid: since the surrounding area was now entirely uninhabited, the organizers were obliged to press for the rapid discovery of a group, even if its activities did not yet quite merit the name of conspiracy. Without waiting for suspicions to be confirmed, they had the alleged conspirators cut down like unripe fruit, and so were able to complete their edifice. It became clear that the architect Kara Houleg was rather better informed about his predecessor Imhotep than might have been supposed, since he undertook to explain to his sovereign that it would be proper, in the light of tradition, to place a pyramidion on the summit. So they set off with great guffaws to find a skull of unusual shape. As they found none, they suddenly thought of one of the camp-followers called Mongka, an idiot with an oversize head. The defective was summoned and told: "We're going to make you into a prince!" After cutting off his head, they poured molten lead over it to general amusement before sticking it right on top of the stack.

When Timur's army had moved away from Isfahan, leaving its frightful monument in the midst of the steppe, the whole area seemed even more deserted. Crows and jackdaws wheeled over the skullstack, then swooped down to pick at the eyes of the heads that the builders had taken care to place face outward, as Kara Houleg had instructed.

Freezing temperatures came earlier than expected that year. Rain had long since washed away all trace of blood, and quite soon powdery frost covered the slopes of the stack, especially the northern slope. No damage was done to it by winter storms, except for the lightning that was apparently attracted by the leaded head of the idiot Mongka. To everyone's amazement it made not the slightest scratch to the head itself but remelted the lead, which spread down to form spikes on each side of the forehead and also trickled into the eye-sockets, giving them that look of cloudy vacuousness characteristic of the faces of the gods.

Snow twice covered the pyramid that winter. Toward the spring, when the March winds restored the stack's dark hue, head and face hair could be seen once again. Pilgrims trekking across Asia were mostly horrified at the sight, but those who knew the history of the world stated that the hair had not appeared by chance: four thousand years earlier, they said, a prophet and martyr had foretold that the pyramid would one day grow a beard. At least, that was the kind of story that you could hear being put about. There were even songs about it; but no one suspected that the legend originated in the chance discovery of a papyrus used to copy down the inquisitor's interrogation of Setka the Idiot.

Meanwhile, the wild beasts of the steppes prowled about at night, and by day, their snouts stuffed with clumps of hair snatched from Timur's pyramid, they raced with the howling wind across the plateau of Turkmenistan, through the sands of Kandahar, and even farther afield, into the vast Mongolian plain.

He got used to the sight, and on every plain where he set up camp a pile of heads was hastily made. Then, like a Pharaoh, he empowered his sons and grandsons to have their own pyramids, and eventually gave this right to all the generals of his army. As a result many hundreds were made, and they spread such terror as to become an indispensable feature of every campaign that was launched. When each new heap was made—as they were still endowed with eyes, they were called *head piles*—the older ones, made two or three years before, had already been transformed into *skullstacks*. However, though the skulls had only sockets for eyes, they kept their teeth, just as the prophecy had foretold.

In the myriad tents of the army, and even more in the cities and states that it threatened, people spoke of the Isfahan pyramid with such fear and loathing that many reckoned that, even if it was hardly up to the *stonestack* of Cheops in terms of its size, the time it had taken to build, and its lack of antiquity, it was nonetheless the real thing, the Egyptians' old heap being nothing but a paltry, overblown imitation.

The Isfahan pyramid was the one that possessed a straight, firm, and living character. Timur's stack spread instant panic like a thunderclap. It was unaffected by rumors or by flattery, it consumed men's heads in a few hours, in the time it took for a *qatl i amm,* instead of dragging things out over years or decades and making people wade through files and investigations beyond counting, not to mention cuts in the bread ration, anguish, and despair. Its diamantine density gave it its sparkle, its brilliance was in the idea that had governed its construction: and the upshot of all this was that the rhapsodists and subsequently the scholars of Samarkand eventually proclaimed that the first authentic pyramid had arisen in the Isfahan steppe, and that its Egyptian rival was a crude replica of later date. Although this claim may at first have sounded somewhat bizarre, close attention to the ballads of the shamans would have informed you that, since no one could say whether time flowed forward or backward, no one could be sure of the ages of people and things, and thus their order of appearance was even less fixed. In other words, who can tell who is the father and who the son? And so on.

During one of his long marches Timur remembered that Isfahan was not far away from one of his army's flanks, and a sense of foreboding made him want to set eyes upon his pyramid one more time. It now looked a little shriveled. Part of the leaden head of the mental defective had split, and all the tufts of hair on the lower rows had been torn out by wild beasts. But the jawbones were clamped together more tightly than ever. As if the pyramid was threatening, or alternatively provoking, the whole world. He cast a melancholy gaze at the first signs of its decline, and when he was told that it might stay up for another four or maybe five years, but not longer, he sighed. An empty shell far away, somewhere in Egypt, could keep on going after four millennia, and was going to last another forty, whereas this treasure would have a life as short that of as his son Djahangjir, and had but four more years to go.

He turned his head toward where Egypt was supposed to be, and nodded slowly. Patience, he thought. One day he would set out to sweep that state off the face of the earth, together with all its stonestacks. He would dismantle them, especially the tallest, Cheops's stack, and he would replace that grotesque edifice with a skullstack of equal volume, to show everyone which pile was the true pyramid, and which one just a piece of scenery on the world's stage.

But he could not set off just yet. He was intent on his Chinese campaign, and the winter had set in early that year. It was the Year of the Dog, a year he had never liked very much. The Sir Daria was already half frozen over, and he was not feeling at his best. His mind wandered toward impossible projects—for instance, to the time when, a few years earlier, during the Siberian campaign, despite the magicians' terrified prayers, night would not fall, because of what people called the northern lights. That was during a Year of the Rat, and he racked his brains trying to work out the complexities of the calendar; yet his own days and nights had become as misshapen as embryos from incestuous couplings.

He felt feverish, as he had done during the northern lights. He would have liked to concentrate his mind on simpler things, such as remembering to avoid having the first skirmish during a rainstorm, so as not to suffer the consequences that arose at the battle of Sijabkir, when his archers could not target correctly with sodden bows. His mind was drawn to dozens of other concrete and visible topics, but the skullstack interfered with his thinking. He was less obsessed with the dense glint of lead on the idiot's head than with the wire thread that ran through all the skulls, and especially with the lightning that, according to the reports he had received, had darted all the way through, faster than a snake . . .

A thought that connected the wire that linked the heads to lightning and to his own orders was struggling to take shape in his brain, but, as during the Siberian campaign, it never quite managed to come together.

No doubt about it, he had a fever. He expected that death would await him at Otrar, but it could be no more than the mask of death. The death he feared above all others was the one that habitually pursued him on the far edges of his empire, in the untilled lands, the great swampy deserts where reeds were as thinly spread as Mongolian monks.

XVI

Epilogue

Of a Transparent Kind

AFTER Timur's funeral no one cared any longer about
restoring his heaps of skulls. There were more than
nine such piles, constituted of about one million heads, and
they vanished entirely within a few years. Decomposition
of the soft parts of the heads first caused fissures in the
mortar, then the wires rusted, and when they snapped they
brought about the collapse of the whole structure. Winter
hurricanes and more particularly wild animals tore the
rows down one by one, until nothing was left at all. Once
they had been reduced to naught, these edifices became ever
taller and more fearsome in the memory of men. And so it
became possible to judge just how much the mother of
them all, the pyramid of Cheops, had lost by being spared
from destruction.

It remained a prolific childbearer beneath the scorching
sun, but its offspring were not easy to discern. Descendants

cropped up in other countries and in other periods, as
regimes or historical monuments, but it was hard to believe
they had first been conceived in the middle of the Egyptian
desert. They always took on false names, and only on two
occasions did they make the mistake of declaring themselves
openly, like a man removing or accidentally dropping his terrifying mask. The first was Timur the Lame's skullstacks; their
second reappearance took place six hundred years later, in
the land that had previously belonged to the Illyrians and
had now been handed down to their descendants under the
name of Albania. Like the product of a cosmic copulation
such as the Ancients might have imagined—in which sperm
and eggs are dispersed in huge abandon and engender a multitude of creatures or celestial bodies—the old pyramid
spawned not thousands, but hundreds of thousands of little
ones. They were called bunkers, and each of them, however
tiny it may have been in comparison, transmitted all the
terror that the mother of all pyramids had inspired, and all
the madness too. Steel rods were planted in the concrete, following the principle invented long before by Kara Houleg.
The word *Unity* was often inscribed on their loins, showing
that these bunkers were indeed related both to the mother-
pyramid and to the skullstacks, and that the old dream of
connecting all brains to each other by a single idea could only
be achieved by such rods of iron running through people's
heads and making of them a united entity.

Pyramidal phenomena occurred in cycles, without it ever
being possible to determine precisely the timing of their appearance: for no one has ever been able to establish with cer-
tainty whether what happens is the future, or just the past
moving backward, like a crab. People ended up accepting

that maybe neither the past nor the future were what they were thought to be, since both could reverse their direction of travel, like trams at a terminus.

One morning a fair-haired tourist who was taking photographs of the pyramid made a wish: that the monument should become quite transparent, so that everything inside—the sarcophagi, the mummies, the indecipherable puzzle—would be visible, as through a wall of glass. Day was breaking, the pyramid began to go hazy, and the tourist could feel a shiver in his soul with each passing minute, as if he were at a spiritualist seance and about to take a snapshot of a ghost.

He developed his roll of film the same evening, and the pyramid really did look like a glass house, except that on one edge, near the ninth row on the northeast slope, you could see some kind of blemish. He took the film out of the developer, put it back in . . . to a depth of a thousand, of four thousand years . . . but when he finally took it out, the blemish was still there. It was not, as he had first thought, a fault in the film. It was a bloodstain that neither water nor acid would ever wash clean.

Tirana–Paris, 1988-1992